RAVES FO
THE BETTER TO KIS_ YOU WITH
SERIES

"*The Better to Kiss You With* is a heady paranormal romance with a Canadian Gothic atmosphere. Cherry blossoms bloom in a moody, misty spring while terrible notes turn up and computers can haunt more than any presence."

—Friend of Dorothy Wilde Book Blog

"4 ½ stars… It was so well written that I never once doubted it. The last part of the book was very exciting and full of threat and suspense."

—Inked Rainbow Reads Reviews on *The Better to Kiss You With*

"4 ½ stars… I really enjoyed the writing style of Ms. Osgood and hope to read more by her in the future. Her voice was so clear and the emotions she brings forth are so rich. I kind of don't want this book to end."

—Molly Lolly Book Reviews on *The Better to Kiss You With*

"… a delicious mix of urban fantasy and queer feminist romance."

—Autostraddle on *Huntsmen*

"Blazing hot..."

—Just Love Reviews on *Huntsmen*

"... gosh did I love every intense second of it."

—G. Jacks Writes Blog on *Huntsmen*

The Better To Kiss You With

Michelle Osgood

interlude 🧩 press · new york

Published by Interlude Press
www.interludepress.com
BOOK AND COVER DESIGN by CB Messer
COVER ART by Monika Gross

10 9 8 7 6 5 4 3 2 1

interlude ✦ press • new york

To ECHC.

"All stories are about wolves."

—Margaret Atwood

Chapter One |

THE THIRD TIME HER PHONE chimed to remind her to take out the garbage, Deanna Scott heaved a sigh and paused her episode of *Orphan Black*. She dislodged Arthur, who looked up at her with sad eyes as only a golden retriever can, then disentangled herself from the blanket and moved the bowl of popcorn to the table. If she didn't take the garbage out now, she never would.

Grabbing her keys, the garbage and an ugly sweater that wouldn't do much to protect her from the Vancouver rain but would at least cover the threadbare tank top she was wearing, Deanna shoved her feet into her boots and unlocked the door. Behind her, Arthur gave a plaintive whine.

"Quiet, Arthur. It's raining, so if you come with me you'll get wet. And you're going to want to sit on the couch while we finish that episode. And I don't want to cuddle with a wet dog. We've been over this," she told him firmly.

At the sound of her voice, Arthur's tail gave a hopeful sweep against the hardwood.

"I'm only going out back. It won't be exciting."

Arthur raised his butt off the floor, asking for permission to come, and when she didn't stop him he bounded over. His whole body wriggled happily.

"Fine, but I'm not going to share the couch with you after." She meant it this time. He could sit on the rug. He should be sitting on the rug anyway. Couches were for people, not dogs.

Deanna opened her front door and let Arthur go down the hall as she locked up behind them. She caught up with him at the stairs and followed him down the seven flights.

Outside it was dark and wet, and, as rain started to run down her face, Deanna wished she'd taken a jacket with an actual hood instead of her floppy old sweater. Her unruly blonde curls would be impossible to comb out after they got wet. Arthur was unperturbed by the weather; his tail waved as he led the way around the corner of their large brick apartment building to the garbage bins at the back.

Deanna held her breath as she lifted the lid on the nearest bin and tossed the bag inside before she darted a couple of steps away to suck in another breath of the damp air. She was sure none of her neighbors actually disposed of rotting corpses in the communal garbage bins, but with a building this size they smelled rank no matter what. For the hundredth time she wondered if she should send an email to the landlord about bumping the garbage collection up from only once every two weeks.

Deanna pulled her sweater tighter around her body and called for Arthur to stop sniffing at the bottom of another bin for rats, or god knew what else dogs found so attractive about garbage, and walked back along the side of the building. The jangle of his collar let her know that Arthur was hurrying to catch up, terrified as always of being left behind.

She unlocked the front door and held it open to let him go through, then rolled her eyes when he stopped in the middle of the small lobby and gave a thorough shake, sending beads of water flying through the air. His paws left wet tracks on the dark wooden stairs as he climbed;

she'd have to give him a rubdown with a towel before she could let him back on the couch, which, she knew, she'd be coerced into doing when he turned his puppy eyes on her.

"I should have listened to my mother and got a cat," she muttered as she rounded the final flight of stairs. She couldn't hear Arthur's collar anymore but assumed he'd be waiting at the door to the seventh floor as he always did. When she reached their floor, though, he wasn't there. Frowning, Deanna pushed open the door and glanced down the hallway. It was possible that a neighbor had left the heavy door open, and Arthur had gone all the way to their apartment. But the hallway was empty.

Though she knew it was silly, there was a quick spark of alarm in her chest. Arthur was a good dog. He knew to stay close to her. "Arthur?" she called, worry making her voice rise.

"I think I've got him," a deeper voice replied. Deanna whirled around to look behind her before she realized the voice was coming from the next level up.

She crossed the landing and hurried up the next flight of stairs, then turned the corner to see Arthur sprawled at the top of the eighth floor landing with his tail thumping in giddy appreciation of the belly rub he was receiving.

"Oh, I'm sorry," Deanna said to the person who was bent over her dog and sending him into paroxysms of joy. The stranger had dark hair cropped close on both sides, with a longer shock that fell over the face, and a man's button-up fitted tightly over broad shoulders. When Deanna spoke, the stranger looked up.

At first Deanna guessed the person was a guy, a college kid whose jaw was still stubbornly smooth, but as the figure straightened Deanna caught the soft hint of breasts under the shirt. Suddenly she could see the thick frame of lashes around a pair of amber eyes, and the feminine curve to lips tugged into a wide and rueful grin. Deanna hastily tacked several years onto the stranger's age: not a kid at all, but someone closer to her own twenty-six. Deanna swallowed, her throat uncomfortably dry, and desperately wished she was wearing something other than a faded pair of pajama pants and the ugliest sweater she owned.

"It's okay." The stranger continued to pet Arthur, who'd closed his eyes in bliss. She gave a self-conscious sort of shrug. "Dogs like me."

Deanna could see why. She wished those long fingers were stroking *her* belly. The thought had her flushing, mortified, and she spared a moment of thanks that the woman's attention was on Arthur so she couldn't see the pink in Deanna's cheeks. "Come on, Arthur," she managed.

Arthur cracked open an eye but made no move to obey Deanna.

"Arthur," Deanna repeated, putting a little more force in her tone, "come on, let's go back home. I'm really sorry," she said helplessly when Arthur just wriggled closer to the attractive stranger. "He normally listens a lot better than this."

The woman stood up, and Arthur scrabbled to his feet beside her. "Go on," she said, looking down at Arthur. She gave his head a final pat. With a soulful doggy sigh, Arthur pressed his wet nose into her hand and moved down the stairs past Deanna, where he turned back with an expectant look as if to ask why Deanna hadn't followed.

Deanna returned his look with a scowl and then turned back. "Thanks." She wasn't sure what the gorgeous stranger had done that was any different than what *she* had done, but it had clearly worked.

"No worries," the woman ran a hand casually through her short hair, and Deanna caught herself glancing down as the movement lifted the woman's shirt up, baring a brief flash of skin above the waistband of her jeans. Deanna pressed her lips together and moved down a step; she needed to put some space between them before she fell to the floor at the stranger's feet and begged to be petted as well.

"I'll, um," Deanna said as she edged down another step, "see you around then?" She gave an awkward wave and, not waiting for a response, fled down the stairs after Arthur.

On the seventh floor she pulled open the door and headed straight toward her apartment, not stopping until she and Arthur were safely ensconced inside.

As she leaned against the closed door, Deanna shut her eyes and let her head fall back against the wood. The first hot girl she'd met in months, and she acted like a total dork. Plus, Deanna confirmed when she opened her eyes and caught sight of her reflection in the mirror, her blonde hair was a frizzy mess from the rain, and the old wire-rimmed glasses she was wearing over her soft green eyes made her look like someone's spinster aunt. With a groan, she dropped the keys into the dish under the mirror and walked into the living room, toeing off her shoes as she went.

Arthur was already curled up on the couch. She shoved him over and got a handful of damp fur in the process. Deanna flopped down beside him and picked up the remote. With any luck, the woman was just visiting a friend and Deanna wouldn't actually see her around.

Chapter Two |

TWO WEEKS LATER, ON HER way home from lunch with her friend Nathan, Deanna stopped to pick up fresh flowers. She was terrible at keeping plants alive. The herb garden she'd once thought so inspired had lasted a pitiful three weeks. Despite that, she loved having green things in her home, and the pop of color the flowers gave was too cheerful to resist. Besides, fresh-cut flowers were already dying, so all she had to do was arrange them prettily in a vase with some water and enjoy their last few days on earth. Which, now that she thought of it, was actually really morbid.

Deanna glanced at her bundle of orange tulips and sent them a mental apology.

She crossed the street to her building and fished her keys from her purse. She was glad that she hadn't needed the umbrella she'd left behind.

Since she'd run into the woman on the eighth floor—or, rather, since *Arthur* had run into her—Deanna had been more careful with her appearance when she left her apartment. She hadn't done anything drastic, but when she went out to take Arthur for a walk she made sure to add a bit of color to her lips and, if she was in sweatpants, she wore the ones without any holes. It wasn't that she expected to see the woman again, and she definitely wasn't looking for her. Deanna just wanted to feel a little less grubby if she did happen to see her again. That was all. Besides, Heather from across the hall was probably sick of Deanna's shockingly vast collection of shapeless loungewear.

It had been over a year since her last relationship, her roommate was a dog and she worked from home as a moderator on an online game. It wasn't as if Deanna had any reason to spend her time in clothes that weren't perfectly comfortable. She did own plenty of nice clothes; it was just that she didn't need pants, or even underwear, to do her job. Her "real people" clothes tended to stay tucked into the back of her closet unless she was out with friends. Or, say, on a date. Not that she expected to have a date in the near future, but, hey, a girl could dream. And, in the absence of a date, Deanna had decided to wear one of her cute dresses to meet Nathan for lunch.

She was grateful for that decision when she went up the first flight of stairs to the lobby and once again found herself in front of the stranger from the eighth floor. She was crouched again, not for an ecstatic dog, but struggling with several large bags of groceries, one of which had split open.

"Oh, let me help." Deanna moved forward before she had a chance to think. She knelt and began to gather up the fallen packages.

"It's fine, I don't need—" the dark-haired woman began, but she cut herself off when it became apparent that Deanna had already re-bagged the groceries nearest to her. "Thank you," she said, as she added the last of her fallen groceries to the other, unbroken bags.

"No problem," Deanna said with an easy smile. "I owe you one anyway. You found my dog, remember?"

The woman gave a short laugh, then rubbed her hand over her mouth. "I think I'm the reason you were missing him in the first place, so if we're keeping track, between that and this," she nodded at the groceries, "it looks like I owe you two."

The stranger's eyes were the warm brown of good bourbon and nearly as intoxicating. "Let me help you carry those up, and you can make it three." Deanna flashed a smile. She was *so* much better at flirting when she'd combed her hair that day and knew for a fact that she was wearing deodorant. "I'm Deanna, by the way."

"Deanna," the woman repeated, in her low, melodic voice, catching Deanna's gaze and holding it before she rose to her feet. "I'm Jamie Martineau. And thanks, but it's all right, I can take them myself."

Since it was clearly not humanly possible for her to carry three overflowing bags of groceries, Deanna waved away Jamie's protest and reached down for the bag closest to her.

"Holy crap, no wonder the other one broke!" Deanna exclaimed as she struggled to hoist the bag. She couldn't imagine how Jamie had carried four of them at once. Putting the tulips on top of the bag, Deanna used both hands to lift it.

"These are lighter?" Jamie offered, though her biceps flexed impressively as she picked up the remaining two bags. They must have been a lot lighter than the bag Deanna was struggling with, because, although the bags looked ready to burst, Jamie didn't seem to be straining under their weight as she led the way up the stairs.

By the third floor, sweat had gathered under Deanna's arms, and she was deeply grateful for her deodorant. Was she seriously this out of shape? She wasn't the type of person who liked to work out, but she still had to climb these stairs with her own groceries often enough. She was never more than a little winded by the time she got to the seventh floor, even if she had to cart up Arthur's giant bag of dog food.

"Almost there," Jamie called. If she could hear Deanna's panting, she politely ignored it.

When they finally reached the eighth floor, Deanna felt as if she'd climbed a mountain carrying a month's worth of canned goods in her arms.

Deanna had never been on the eighth floor, but she'd assumed it would look just like the rest of the building. Her assumption proved wrong when, as she followed Jamie down the hall, she was distracted enough by the long expanse of door-free wall to pull her attention from the pair of loose-fitting boyfriend jeans that was doing Jamie's butt a great many favors.

"How many apartments are on this floor?" Deanna asked, only slightly breathless and trying to keep the thread of envy out of her voice.

"Three. Mine's the one on the end."

Great. Deanna would have groaned if she had the energy left. The hottie was her upstairs neighbor. Did that mean she could hear Deanna's occasional—okay, habitual—Taylor Swift dance parties? Or the sound of the horror movies Deanna sometimes decided it was a good idea to watch alone at night, and which always wound up scaring the crap out of her? Deanna was certain she'd actually screamed a few times when something jumped out on the TV screen.

Jamie somehow managed to get the key in the lock and open her door while balancing the two bags. Deanna eased the bag she was carrying onto her hip and followed Jamie.

The place was easily triple the size of Deanna's. As Deanna stepped awkwardly out of her flats, not wanting to put down the bag in case she wasn't able to convince her arms to pick it up again, she cast a covetous glance around. Where Deanna's floors were hardwood, Jamie had creamy white carpet. Before Deanna followed Jamie into the open-concept kitchen, she closed her eyes for a second of bliss as her toes sank in.

The walls in the living room were painted dove-gray and hung with photographs in various sizes, all framed in thick black wood. A pretty teal couch with coordinating armchairs dominated the space, and Deanna assumed that a short hallway led off to the bedroom and bathroom.

"Have you been in the building long? This place is great. You won't believe how tiny mine is," Deanna commented as she finally set the bag down on the kitchen island.

She put her flowers to the side and began to take groceries out of the bag and put them on the counter as she continued her appraisal. "I love the pictures you've got up. Is that your family? They look super fun." A jumble of colors and sizes and smiles, the faces in the photos on Jamie's wall beamed. "Are you all from here?"

When she finally pulled her attention away from the apartment, Deanna had emptied nearly the entire bag of groceries, and Jamie was looking at her strangely from where she'd put her still-packed bags on the kitchen table. Oops.

"I've been here for a few months," was Jamie's only response, and Deanna wilted around the edges. Her friend Nathan always told her that the "full-on-Deanna" could be too intense sometimes, and she was beginning to understand what he'd meant. Not only had she ignored Jamie's insistence that she didn't need help with her groceries, but Deanna had then barged into her apartment and was doing everything short of borrowing Jamie's pajamas to make herself at home.

"I'm sorry, you can probably handle things from here." Deanna gave a weak laugh, stepped back from the counter and clasped her hands behind her back.

"Thank you for your help," Jamie said, not contradicting what Deanna had said. It stung, but Deanna figured she'd had it coming. Jamie shifted to lean back against her counter; the movement looked almost forced, and Deanna realized she was still standing unwelcome in the middle of a stranger's apartment.

"Of course." Trying not to look as though she was fleeing, Deanna shoved her feet back into her flats and let herself out, closing the door firmly behind her.

In her own apartment, and after Arthur had given her an enthusiastic welcome back that left her with dog hair all over her dress, Deanna went into the kitchen and poured herself a large glass of cold water. What she really needed, she thought with a mental groan, was a cold shower. She took a sip of water, and then pressed the side of the glass to her still-heated cheeks. What was it about Jamie that left her so flustered?

Okay, it probably had something to do with Jamie's wide mouth and clever hands, and the impressive way Jamie's muscles had worked under her T-shirt as she'd climbed the stairs.

Maybe Deanna just needed to get laid. Or get off. Maybe, she tapped a finger pensively against the glass, an orgasm or two would exorcize her increasingly embarrassing crush.

Emboldened by the idea, Deanna took another long drink and went into the main room. One of the downsides of not living with a roommate was that she couldn't afford an apartment with a separate bedroom, so a single room had to double as both her living room and her bedroom. The sofa bed was one of the world's greatest inventions.

Deanna put the glass down on the coffee table and ducked into the bathroom. She pulled open a drawer on the bottom of her wardrobe, another concession to the small space, to find her vibrator. After untangling it from several pairs of underwear, she pushed the drawer closed with her foot and returned to the living room, putting the vibrator down beside the water glass before she turned to pull the curtains across the window.

As she was bending to pull off the couch cushions, there was a knock outside. Arthur rose from his bed in her tiny entranceway and stood at the door, tail wagging. It didn't sound like the knock had been on Deanna's door, but Arthur looked as if he expected company. Frowning, she crossed the room and pushed Arthur out of her way, then stood on tiptoe to look out the peephole.

Across the hall, at her neighbor Heather's door, stood Jamie. She seemed to be holding something, but it was between her body and Heather's door, so Deanna couldn't see what. Now that she knew no one was at her own door, Deanna knew she should quit watching—spying, really—but she couldn't bring herself to stop.

Did Jamie know Heather? How was it that two of her nearest neighbors were friends and Deanna hadn't ever seen them together?

Deanna's workplace was online, so she could work from anywhere, which meant she was home often enough that she ought to have noticed.

Heather opened the door, and Jamie stepped back.

"Yes?" Heather asked.

"Hi, sorry," Jamie rubbed a hand over the back of her neck and, despite herself, Deanna pressed closer to the door so she could hear their conversation better. "I'm actually looking for Deanna."

"Who?" Heather frowned, and Deanna dropped her forehead against the door in front of her. Heather was pushing ninety and, while she was probably more physically fit than Deanna, she occasionally had what she'd call "senior moments."

"Oh, um." Jamie's ears pinked. "I think she lives on this floor? Pretty, blonde, sometimes wears glasses. She has a dog?"

Heather nodded knowingly. "Oh, of course. You mean Deanna. She's just across the hall." Heather pointed, and Jamie turned, and Deanna scrambled back from the door.

"Thank you," Deanna heard Jamie say and then heard Heather's door close. Though if she knew Heather at all, the older woman would be pressed up against her door just as Deanna had been. At the sound of footsteps in the hall, Arthur's tail began to wag furiously. Jamie knocked.

Deanna stood, frozen, for one long heartbeat before her brain kicked back into gear. She muscled Arthur out of the way and turned the lock. She was about to swing the door open, thinking she should make the best of this moment and invite Jamie in for a glass of wine, but as she glanced over her shoulder to make sure her living room was presentable, Deanna caught sight of her vibrator, flamboyantly purple in the center of her coffee table.

Oh, shit.

Because Jamie was just inches away and would be able to hear the hesitation between Deanna unlocking the door and opening it, Deanna twisted the knob and pulled it open just a fraction. Beside her,

Arthur gave an annoyed whine and tried to wriggle past. Deanna had to slam her hip into the doorframe to block him.

"Hi," she said, flashing a smile as she prayed that Jamie wouldn't be able to see inside.

"Hi." Jamie's thick eyebrows furrowed as Arthur tried again to get past Deanna and say his own hello.

"Arthur's covered in, um, flea powder," Deanna improvised. "Otherwise I'd… well. Anyway. What can I do for you?" Deanna had to tilt her head up ever so slightly to meet Jamie's eyes, and for the briefest moment she could have sworn Jamie's eyes dropped to Deanna's lips.

"You forgot these." Jamie held out the bundle of tulips, and Deanna blushed.

Deanna took the flowers and forced herself to take a slow breath. She was not a flustered disaster. She was calm and collected and—she reminded herself with a hint of delight—the person she had a total crush on thought she was pretty. She could do this one thing without making a fool of herself. "Thank you," she said gracefully.

"You're welcome." Jamie had no reason to linger at Deanna's doorway, not when she'd already given Deanna her flowers, and Deanna had already offered an excuse for not inviting her in, but she hadn't moved.

Deanna clamped down on the stream of mindless babble that had flown to the tip of her tongue and tried to stay relaxed, a tricky feat, since Arthur still hadn't given up trying to push past her legs. God, she wished she'd left her vibrator in the drawer. If she could invite Jamie in, maybe she could find out why Jamie was looking at Deanna as if she was a question and Jamie didn't know the answer.

Deanna's pulse quickened as Jamie made no move to leave, and when Jamie's lips parted Deanna's breath caught in her throat.

"I— left the milk out," Jamie said finally, drawing back. Deanna ignored the sudden ache in the center of her chest and curled her fingers around the door. She wanted nothing more than to reach out and stop Jamie from leaving.

"You should put it away," Deanna agreed. Jamie gave a slow nod and, with a wave, turned and headed down the hallway.

Beside Deanna, Arthur gave a long, unhappy whine and finally quit trying to press past her. "I know, baby," Deanna soothed, closing the door and petting his head. "I know."

DEANNA TOOK ARTHUR ON A long walk that evening. He was overjoyed when she steered them toward the large forested park that separated the university from the rest of the city. Since Arthur was nearly impossible to drag out of the woods in under an hour, the adventure usually took at least two, and Deanna only took him a few times a month.

At the edge of the trees, she unclipped Arthur's leash. Technically this spot wasn't an off-leash area, but Arthur rarely ventured far out of her sight. And if he did, he was more than ready to come back when she called.

Arthur barked happily and bounded playfully around her before racing into the woods.

Wishing she'd remembered to bring her iPod, Deanna tucked her hands into her pockets and headed down the path. This part of the park wasn't isolated. It was close enough to one of the main roads to the university that the orange glow of streetlights filtered through the trees to her left, and Deanna didn't have too much trouble seeing the path. Farther into the trees it grew darker, but Deanna's eyes had adjusted enough that she could see where she was going. It helped that Arthur's coat was so light in color that he tended to stand out like a wriggling and occasionally muddy beacon.

It wasn't raining, at least. Deanna was grateful for that, but the air was still damp and cool with the threat of it. It lent the woods an eerie feel, as though they were far removed from civilization.

Usually, Deanna enjoyed that feeling. It took her mind off of mundane irritations, such as the obnoxious user she was dealing with on the game she worked for, or the giant crush she had on her sexy upstairs neighbor. Getting into the woods usually allowed her to settle back into herself. Tonight that didn't seem to be working. She was an extrovert, but in her new job she spent a lot less time dealing with people face to face. Somehow, that seemed to make her in-person interactions more emotionally charged rather than less, and she couldn't get what had happened with Jamie out of her head.

Deanna kicked a fallen branch out of her way and tried to relax. She could feel the tension in her face, which meant she'd been holding onto a frown for longer than necessary. She shouldn't be so hung up on something that had happened hours ago. Just because she'd barged into a stranger's apartment and had to be not-so-subtly asked to leave didn't mean she'd die a shriveled old crone with no one but Arthur for company. And said stranger coming to find her afterward to return her forgotten tulips was nothing more than Jamie being neighborly, certainly not an indication that Jamie was as attracted to Deanna as Deanna was to her. Deanna was reading way too much into what was nothing more than an everyday occurrence between two people who happened to live in the same building.

"This is why I don't like crushes. They make me stupid," she muttered as she followed the curve of the trail deeper into the woods.

Arthur popped out of the trees ahead of her and waited on the path as though to signal that he agreed. She made a face at him, and with a snort he ran back into the trees.

"It's fine," she called after him. "Not like I need some friendly reassurance that I'm not a total ass."

Silence greeted her. Even Arthur thought she had been an idiot. Wonderful.

Now that they were farther into the forest, the glow of the waxing moon shone through a break in the trees. Since the light pollution had eased somewhat, Deanna could catch a glimmer of stars. If she went deep enough, following this trail to the amphitheater at the center of the park, she'd be able to see whole constellations. That was an extra hour's walk, though, so Deanna didn't often venture that far.

Nearing the giant stump that Deanna used to mark her and Arthur's usual turn-back point, Deanna realized that it had been too long since Arthur had last doubled back to her.

"You've got to stop doing this to me," she complained, attempting to cover her worry with irritation. "I don't know what your problem is lately. Arthur!" When a rustle of underbrush and the jangle of his dog tags didn't immediately answer her call, she repeated it, louder. "Arthur!"

A dart of panic tightened her throat, and Deanna picked up her pace, her lazy stroll now an urgent half-jog. She'd seen Arthur go into the woods on her right, and it stood to reason that unless he'd looped behind her, he would have come out on the path ahead. Which meant she should have seen him. It was unlikely that he'd have let her get so far ahead that she wouldn't have heard him on the trail behind her. And he knew this was where they turned around. He'd never gone farther down the path without waiting for her at the stump.

Deanna tried to tamp down the feeling that something bad had happened. "Arthur, do not do this to me. I am not kidding." Her hand moved into her jacket pocket, and she touched the edge of her phone, tempted to pull it out and turn on the flashlight app. But if she turned on the light, it would ruin her night vision, and she wasn't too keen on that either.

As silence continued to stretch out, Deanna came to a stop in front of the stump, and turned to stare apprehensively at the great stretch of woods ahead. They were dense, and Arthur would be able to move through them a lot more quickly than she would. If she went into the forest, there was no guarantee that she'd find him. The smart thing would be to go back the way they'd come, moving slowly and loudly so that he could find her. Unless, of course, he was hurt or trapped. And if he was hurt or trapped, then he'd be able to hear her leaving, and what if he thought she was abandoning him?

Deanna chewed on her lower lip; panic rose until she could taste it, hard and metallic, in the back of her throat. Just as she'd made up her mind to do the stupid thing and plunge into the woods, she heard a branch snap followed by a violent rustle of underbrush. Deanna leapt back instinctively as Arthur burst through the trees and made a beeline toward her. His tail was curled tightly between his legs and he must have waded through a mud puddle; his nose and coat were matted with something dark and sticky.

Body trembling, Arthur pressed himself against her legs and whined. Deanna crouched to run a reassuring hand through his fur, grimacing a little at the mud tacky on her fingers. "It's okay, baby. You made it back. Good dog," she soothed as she clipped his leash on.

She had no idea what had frightened him so badly. The occasional coyote wasn't unusual, and it stood to reason that where there was one there were bound to be more. If that's what this was about, Deanna didn't want to stick around to meet them. With Arthur close by her side, she hurried back up the path.

THE ORANGE STREETLIGHTS CAST A peculiar glow on the remainder of their walk through the city, and when they got back to their building, the bright white light of the lobby shone through the glass doors. It illuminated Deanna's hand as she brought her key to the lock. She gasped when she realized that the tacky substance drying on her fingers wasn't mud at all.

She stared at the dark liquid caked under her fingernails. She'd tried to rub most of it off on her jeans, but hadn't managed to do more than smear it. Not wanting to look, but knowing she had to, Deanna looked at Arthur. He was pressed tight against her leg, and Deanna saw with a detached sense of horror that his silky fur was coated with dirt and blood.

Chapter Three |

NATHAN REFILLED HIS GLASS OF beer from the growler.

"I think I know blood when I see it," Deanna pointed out. "It was definitely blood."

Beside her on the floor, Nathan leaned his head back against the couch and, behind the black frames of his glasses, rolled his bright blue eyes. "I'm not saying it wasn't blood. But just, like, blood happens."

"'Blood happens.' You sound like a tampon commercial."

"Not true." Nathan snickered over the top of his glass. "They never use the word 'blood.'"

Deanna choked on a mouthful of wine.

"Anyway," Nathan continued, "it was probably just a dead animal. Dogs love that stuff."

"He wasn't happy, though. He was scared. Something scared him. And Arthur's brave. He doesn't scare easily." Deanna wiped the Pinot Gris from her chin and they both leaned forward to look at Arthur, who was sprawled artlessly on top of his dog bed and snoring loudly. Deanna smothered a giggle with the back of her hand and grabbed the bottle of wine.

"Just don't confuse fantasy with reality. I think your job is messing you up."

Deanna snorted. "*Wolf's Run* is a just game, Nathan. I haven't forgotten that."

"Really? Because you're talking about mysterious bodies torn up in the woods, and if that doesn't sound like werewolves…"

Deanna gave Nathan a shove. "Ha, ha, very funny. I'm not like that weirdo who thinks that werewolves actually exist. It's role-playing. *Playing* being the key word."

For the most part, the players of *Wolf's Run* were a good crowd— with the exception of one user who seemed to think that he actually *was* a werewolf. Apparently, he took offense to the game's depictions of "his species," considering them inaccurate and insulting. The rants had been going on for months, and the situation would have been laughable, except that in the last few weeks his posts had taken on a more threatening tone. Every time Deanna deleted his posts and blocked his username he simply created another account. The *Wolf's Run* team didn't want to block his IP address because IP addresses could be shared by a large number of people, and doing so might block legitimate players from the game. Besides, it was child's play to circumvent a block by logging in from a third-party app or web service, or just logging in from a different location. Deanna could only shut him down and hope that this time he finally gave up.

"Well, then just accept that Arthur found a bunny rabbit or something and decided it would be a good idea to roll around in its mangled corpse."

Deanna shook her head. "You didn't see him. It was a lot of blood." It had taken two desperately unpleasant baths and an entire bottle of shampoo to get Arthur clean. Deanna had had to scrub her bathtub three times before she'd felt comfortable using it again.

Nathan grabbed her hand with his long, thin fingers. "Listen, you're my best friend, and I love you, and I'm sure that it was really terrifying, but I'm also one hundred percent sure that you are blowing this way out of proportion. No more fantasy werewolf role playing nonsense for you."

"Until my shift starts in…" Deanna tapped the screen of her phone. "Ten hours."

"Until then," Nathan agreed and clinked their glasses. "Now, tell me more about your hot neighbor."

Deanna buried her head in her hands and groaned. "It's awful. She's gorgeous. And I can't think around her. Or speak. I turn into a spluttering sixth grader with her first crush."

"That's disgusting and adorable. Tell me more. What's her name?"

Deanna's reply was stopped by the sound of her buzzer. Putting her wine glass on the floor, she pushed herself to her feet. "Pizza's here. Pizza first, and then I will tell you everything."

"Deal." Nathan went to the kitchen for plates as Deanna stepped into a pair of flats and grabbed her wallet. The pizza place they liked best didn't have a website, so she'd ordered old school—phone in an order and pay at delivery. Arthur made a quiet woof as she opened the door, and opened one bleary eye, but made no move to come with her. Deanna made a face at him and closed the door.

Downstairs, she blessed the fact that Mitilini's was edging toward the twenty-first century and had begun using portable debit machines as she handed the delivery guy her credit card; paying with cash had been such a hassle. She and the delivery guy chatted briefly about the weather (rainy, on and off) as they waited for the transmission to go through. Deanna waved away the receipt and balanced the hot pizza in one hand as she slid her card back into her wallet with the other.

It wasn't until she tucked her wallet under her arm and reached down that she remembered she was wearing a dress. Which meant that she didn't have pockets. Which meant that she'd left her keys in their dish beside the door instead of taking them with her.

She could just buzz for Nathan to come down and let her in. He'd bitch about it, but since she was the one with the pizza, she was fairly sure he'd come get her. Moving her wallet to the top of the pizza box so she could reach for the keypad, she punched in the number for her apartment and waited. After three full minutes had passed, she did it again.

Nothing.

Maybe she'd hit the wrong buttons? She was a bit tipsy; Nathan had brought a bottle of her favorite white wine. And she'd never had to buzz into her own apartment, so maybe she'd messed it up somehow.

Leaning closer, she very deliberately entered the code and waited.

"Come onnnnnnn, Nathan," she complained when, minutes later, he still hadn't come pounding down the stairs to let her in. "I could be getting murdered out here for all you know!"

"If you get murdered, can I have the pizza?" someone asked from right behind her. With a squeak, Deanna whirled around, nearly dropping her pizza and sending her wallet flying.

Trying to smother a grin, Jamie retrieved Deanna's wallet. "Locked yourself out?"

Chagrined, Deanna nodded and tried to keep from staring too blatantly at Jamie, who had clearly just returned from a run. Her red shirt was flecked with drops of rain and dark with sweat under her arms and down the cleft between her breasts. Deanna's mouth watered in a way that had nothing to do with the warm pizza in her hands.

Jamie handed Deanna back her wallet before reaching into her pocket for her keys. Deanna resolutely did not look to see if the tight jogging pants hugged Jamie's ass the way she suspected they did, choosing instead to focus on a drop of water that trickled slowly down from the short hair at the nape of Jamie's neck. She wasn't sure if it was a bead of sweat or rain, and for a split second had a vivid image of leaning forward to press her open mouth to Jamie's heated skin to try to find out.

Swallowing hard, Deanna tore her eyes away just as Jamie unlocked the door and pulled it open, allowing Deanna to squeeze in past her. "Thanks," Deanna said once they were both inside. "I forgot my keys, and my ass of a friend apparently decided not to let me back in."

"It's no problem," Jamie assured her, "But…"

Deanna paused on the stairs, an anxious knot forming in her stomach.

"It's going to cost you this time." Jamie shrugged and continued up past Deanna. Jamie's cheeks held the slightest blush of pink, and Deanna wasn't sure if it was the result of her workout, or… something else.

"Cost me what?" Deanna asked faintly, a thousand scenarios running through her mind. Only nine hundred of which were sexual in nature. Lord, she was just a bit too drunk for this to be happening. *Real life is not a porno. Repeat after me. Real life is not a porno.*

"A slice of that pizza. Maybe even two." Jamie stopped at the seventh floor and once again held open the door.

Now Deanna was picturing herself feeding a very naked Jamie a slice of greasy, cheesy pizza and she had to bite back a moan. Drunk Deanna had very little impulse control.

"Yeah, that could—I could—there's enough to share. It's a large pizza," Deanna managed as they moved down the hallway to her apartment. The closer they got to her place, the more Deanna could understand why Nathan hadn't heard the buzzer. He'd found her iPod and cranked Ke$ha up to full volume.

Deanna tried the doorknob and was glad to see that Nathan hadn't locked it, because she wasn't sure he'd have been able to hear her knock over the music. Excruciatingly aware of Jamie behind her, Deanna entered the apartment.

"Could you turn it down?" she hollered as Nathan danced out of the kitchen where he'd been pulling a second growler out of the fridge. Nathan ignored her, shimmying across the room and only coming to a full stop when he caught sight of Jamie.

"Hot," he yelled, winking at Deanna. When she scowled at him he quickly amended. "Hey. I'm Nathan Roberts. The best friend."

"Jamie," Jamie replied dryly.

Shoving the pizza at Nathan, Deanna fixed him with a thin-lipped death glare before she strode over and turned the music way down.

Nathan wasn't bothering to hide his appraisal of Jamie and, when she bent to unlace her sneakers, he waggled his eyebrows at Deanna and gave her an enthusiastic thumbs up.

Deanna ignored him, glancing frantically around and hoping Jamie wouldn't be too unimpressed with the small space.

She had done a decent job decorating the place. With Nathan's help she'd painted the walls a clean white, hanging a couple of tasteful prints on the larger walls. The fresh flowers she enjoyed so much were in whimsically mismatched glass vases throughout the apartment; the splashes of color lent vibrancy to the stained wood shelving. Her large windows, the apartment's best feature, were framed with linen curtains in periwinkle blue. Due to the lack of space in the main room, she and Nathan had pushed the coffee table out of the way so they could sprawl on the floor, but he was already moving it back into place and had dragged out the armchair she had tucked in a corner so there would be enough seats.

Maybe she wouldn't have to murder him after all.

"Do you, um, want a drink?" Deanna asked. "We've got wine or beer. Or water, if you'd rather." She twisted her hands, not sure what to do with them now that she wasn't holding the pizza. Nathan, meanwhile, had helped himself to a slice and was sitting smugly in Deanna's armchair.

"Beer would be great," Jamie said easily, crossing the room. She started to sit down on the couch and then paused and plucked the material of her shirt away from her skin. "I'm sorry. I'm kind of gross. I should probably grab a shower first."

Deanna paused in mid-reach for a pint glass, her brain helpfully providing her with an image of Jamie standing naked with water cascading down her tall, muscled body.

"Deanna's got one," Nathan offered, sounding nothing less than one hundred percent sincere. Deanna changed her mind again. She could definitely kill him.

"It's fine," Deanna grabbed the glass and hurried out of the tiny kitchen. "Really. This couch has seen a lot worse." Oh god, she really needed to just shut up.

Arthur had trailed Jamie into the main room and, as she settled onto the couch, he sat adoringly at her feet with his chin resting on her leg and his tail pounding against the floor. He didn't look when Deanna opened the pizza box and handed Jamie a slice. Deanna rolled her eyes at him and took her empty wine glass into the kitchen for a refill. When she returned, both Nathan and Jamie were eating, apparently comfortable enough that they didn't need to fill the air with the awkward small talk that was bubbling in Deanna's throat.

Deanna would have bet that Nathan had taken the armchair so that she would be forced to share the couch with Jamie, or else sit on the floor like a total dork. Deanna slowly lowered herself onto the couch and smoothed her skirt over her legs before finally taking a bite of the pizza.

"We were just talking about Deanna's job," Nathan informed Jamie as she took a second slice. "And how it's making her paranoid."

"It's not making me paranoid," Deanna said crossly, trying to convey to Nathan that he should please just shut up, *now*.

"It is," Nathan confirmed around a mouthful of pizza. "Like when we found out that Netflix had all nine seasons of the *X-Files*. For like a year after that Dee was convinced every weird light she saw in the sky was a UFO. 'I want to believe.'" He gave his best Mulder impression.

Jamie laughed. "I'm sorry—what do you do?" she asked Deanna.

They were sitting so close on Deanna's small couch that Deanna could see a light dusting of freckles over Jamie's nose. Deanna wanted to press her lips against each one in turn. She took a hasty gulp of wine before replying. "I'm a content moderator for a role playing game, one of the ones where you download the app and can play from any device in real time."

"Oh, that sounds cool." Jamie leaned forward, clearly interested.

A little flustered with Jamie's full attention on her, Deanna took another drink of wine. "There's a website as well—with profiles and message boards, and that's where most of the game plot takes place. With the app we've mapped out Vancouver and, well, it's a lot like *Ingress*. There are different teams—'packs'—and the goal is to control as much territory as possible."

"It is actually super fun." Nathan grabbed himself another slice of pizza. "You can claim whole areas of the city, and the more members of your pack who claim the same area, the stronger your pack's right to it is. Depending on what's happening with the game plot, some areas are worth more than others. I really need to get back into playing," he mumbled around a mouthful of cheese.

"Nathan gets really into gaming for the, like, three weeks between when one relationship ends and another begins," Deanna confided to Jamie.

"Hey." Nathan raised his middle finger.

Deanna pretended she hadn't seen it. "*Wolf's Run* is a fantasy game and role playing and strategy all in one. We're pretty popular cross-genre."

"I don't understand. Why would that make you paranoid?" Jamie directed her question at Deanna, but glanced at Nathan who leaned forward gleefully in his chair.

"Dee left out the best part," he scolded, eyes gleaming. "The teams are called 'packs' because in the game all the players are werewolves."

Beside Deanna, Jamie choked on her beer, and Deanna mentally face-palmed. Was Nathan trying to make her sound like the world's biggest nerd?

"And our Dee," Nathan continued, willfully oblivious, "is confusing the plot of the game with real life. In *Wolf's Run* some of the packs are anti-human, which means that the occasional human corpse turns up ravaged by 'wild animals.' When that happens, it means all of the players need to be extra careful. Claiming territory becomes harder, because now having multiple players in the same real-life location is a risk, not an asset. With a dead body humans are on alert. It's really fun," he added. "But Dee might be taking it too seriously."

"I'm not taking it too seriously. I don't believe in werewolves, Nathan, come on." Deanna gave an exasperated sigh and watched for Jamie's reaction, but Jamie was avoiding looking at either of them as she reached for another slice.

"I'm not the one freaking out because she thinks she found a dead body," Nathan pointed out.

"I don't think *I* found one," Deanna had to rise to the bait. "I think Arthur did."

As one, all three of them looked down at Arthur.

He yawned.

"Dogs like dead things." Jamie shrugged, giving Arthur's head a stroke. "I'm sure it was just an animal."

"I don't know, with a full moon coming up it could totally have been an out-of-control werewolf!" Nathan growled and tore viciously into his slice of pizza, splattering himself with tomato sauce.

Deanna stuck out her tongue, and, after a moment of baffled silence, Jamie shook her head with a silent chuckle and took another drink of beer.

Nathan wiped his face with the rose-printed paper napkin Deanna had tossed his way. "Anyway, Jamie, Deanna said you're new to the building. What brought you to your humble abode?" He gestured to the ceiling above them, betraying that he and Deanna had discussed her upstairs neighbor's more impressive digs.

Jamie seemed unfazed. "I just moved to the city. I'm doing my master's in race and gender studies at the university."

"No way." Nathan grinned. "I work at the university library, so if you ever need a hand finding research materials or anything, let me know."

"Thank you, I will." Jamie clinked her glass against Nathan's offered one.

"Well, it's been fun." Nathan downed the rest of his beer in one swallow, rose to his feet, and ignored the beseeching look Deanna sent his way. "I've got to work bright and early tomorrow, so I'd better head out. Thanks for the pizza, Dee," he called as he dumped his dishes in the sink before going the door. "It was nice to meet you, Jamie."

"Yeah, you too."

Deanna forced a smile and stood to walk Nathan out. "You're an ass," she hissed through her teeth.

"You love me." He winked. "Have fun and play safe!"

Deanna locked the door behind him, sucking in a quick breath to steady herself before going back into the main room and curling back into her seat on the couch.

"Sorry, if I crashed your dinner." Jamie toyed with the edge of her cushion, awkward for the first time since she'd come in. Deanna reacted on instinct, stilling Jamie's hand with her own.

"You didn't, really." Jamie's skin was warm, and Deanna's palm tingled at the contact. She wondered what would happen if she shifted her light grip and tangled her fingers between Jamie's longer ones. The air between them felt thick, and with an unsteady breath, Deanna drew her hand back. "I've known Nathan since we were both in grade school." Her tongue was clumsy as she forced herself to continue speaking as though nothing had changed. "So it's not like it was a date or anything." God, why had she said that?

"That's good." Jamie hadn't moved her hand and when she looked up her eyes met Deanna's. Deanna felt her mouth go dry and she reached blindly for her glass of wine, then tore her gaze away from Jamie and took a hasty swallow.

"Is it just you upstairs, or…?" Subtle.

"Just me." Jamie settled against the back of the couch. "It's a lot of space for one person, I know," she said with a trace of apology in her voice. Vancouver, like most major cities, was suffering through a longstanding housing crisis, and it seemed almost impossibly decadent to have an apartment that big for just one person.

"You should get a dog," Deanna suggested, trying to regain some composure. "I mean, Arthur obviously loves you." As though he agreed, Arthur's tail thumped against the hardwood.

Jamie scratched his ears, but made a noncommittal noise. "Maybe one day. With school I'm not really home on a regular schedule, and since it's just me it doesn't seem fair."

That was one of the things Deanna liked best about her new job, being able to spend as much time with Arthur as she wanted, even though it seemed Arthur would be more than happy to move in with Jamie without so much as a backward glance. *You and me both, buddy.*

"So, do you know many people here?"

Jamie shook her head. "I'm just starting grad school, so it's mostly seminars and research for my thesis. Which means you, Nathan and Arthur," she added with a self-deprecating smile, "make about a dozen. If you count Heather and the cashier at the grocery store."

"You'll have to come out with us sometime, then," Deanna found herself saying, though what she wanted to say was *me, you should come out with me sometime.* "There's a pub trivia night we like to go to—it sounds lame, but, um, it's actually a lot of fun."

"I'd like that."

"Great." Deanna could feel herself blushing and she looked away, filling her glass with the last of the wine. "I'll let you know when the next one is."

"I'll give you my number." Jamie held out her hand, and it took Deanna a second to realize that she was waiting for Deanna's phone. Deanna opened a new contact tab and handed it over.

"And if you ever need anyone to let Arthur out or something, let me know."

"Thanks, I'll keep that in mind."

Jamie handed Deanna back her phone and then stood, setting her empty glass down on the table. "It's late. I should go."

"Oh." Deanna looked down at the screen and saw that it was nearing midnight. "Yeah, you probably have to get up for school, or... whatever."

"I appreciate the pizza and the beer."

Deanna gave a crooked smile. "Hey, I owed you one."

"Well, we only agreed on pizza." Jamie pointed out as she walked to the door. "So I guess now I owe you a drink."

"At least one," Deanna agreed, rising to follow Jamie.

"Thanks again." Jamie lingered in the open door, and Deanna caught her bottom lip in her teeth, wondering if... but Jamie just held her gaze for one steady beat before closing the door firmly behind her.

Deanna waited until she was sure Jamie was all the way down the hall and would be on her way up the stairs to the eighth floor before she gave in to an incredulous laugh.

Before she forgot, she picked up her phone and sent Jamie a text, just so Jamie would have her number as well.

This is Deanna & Arthur from downstairs! She added the puppy emoticon and, after a brief deliberation, a flower as well. Because flowers were pretty and Jamie had said—not directly to Deanna, but still—that Deanna was pretty, and Deanna didn't think it would hurt to remind her of that.

Chapter Four |

"Wow," Deanna said, still laughing. "I can't believe you knew that there are thirty-seven subspecies of *Canis lupus*. I mean, who knows that?"

They were walking home from Darby's Public House after trivia night, and their teammates had headed in other directions or bummed a ride from Nathan.

"Since that was about the only answer I got right all night, I wouldn't be too impressed," Jamie demurred.

"No one else knew it, though." Deanna shook her head, exhilarated at their win. The night was chilly but clear, and although neither of them had gloves on they both walked with their hands at their sides, when it would have been easiest to tuck their cold fingers into their pockets. The narrow sidewalk meant that they could either walk one behind the other or, as they were, close enough that with every other step Deanna felt Jamie's arm graze her own.

It was imagined, Deanna knew, but she could almost swear she felt heat at every accidental touch. And the touches weren't accidental. Not entirely. She hadn't been sure if her attraction to Jamie had been reciprocated; tonight had definitely confirmed that it was.

They'd spent the night beside each other, squished thigh to thigh in a small booth with five of Deanna's friends, and even when Max ducked out as soon as the quiz had ended, leaving Jamie with room to move over, she hadn't moved away.

She'd stayed, pressed long and lean against Deanna's side, as they'd enjoyed the free pitcher their win had earned them. Hyper-aware of the press of Jamie's leg against her own, the light fabric of her dress and Jamie's jeans all that was between them, Deanna had found it difficult to follow the conversation. Once Jamie had leaned back, casually, and there'd been the light touch of an arm against Deanna's back. Nathan had met her eyes across the table and quickly, secretly grinned before asking their teammate Sadie how her house-hunting was going.

Deanna had let the conversation wash over her then, nursing the rest of her beer, and, after several moments of agonizing internal debate, had slowly leaned back. She'd given Jamie plenty of time to move her arm, if she'd wanted to, but apparently Jamie hadn't. It was as though Deanna was reliving her first childhood crush all over again as she felt Jamie's arm warm and steady against her shoulders.

Now, as they walked home in the dark, Deanna decided it was time to stop beating around the bush. The next time Jamie's hand brushed her own she caught the other woman's fingers. Jamie didn't hesitate. Her fingers wrapped firmly around Deanna's own, and Deanna was sure that without that solid grip she'd have floated straight up into the night sky.

She ducked her head to hide her grin, and caught Jamie's glance out of the corner of her eye. Deanna should say something, probably. But it was so unbearably sweet to just walk hand in hand that she couldn't bring herself to speak.

They walked the final blocks to their building in silence, and it was the furthest thing from uncomfortable as Jamie's thumb slid casually over Deanna's wrist. The light touch sent Deanna's senses skittering until it felt as if all the nerves in her body had gathered in that one spot.

When they reached their building, and Jamie pulled her hand away to reach for her keys, Deanna had to take a deep breath of the cool air to keep from pushing Jamie against the glass doors and taking a fistful of Jamie's short hair so she could drag Jamie's mouth down to hers. As though Jamie could read Deanna's mind, she cast a glance back over her shoulder. A gleam of heat in her eyes had every muscle in Deanna's body pulled tight. Deanna tried to maintain a neutral expression, but the knowing tilt in Jamie's chin nearly undid her.

Passing through the lobby, Deanna caught her reflection in the mirrored panel of the wall: her cheeks were flushed, and the brightness in her green eyes made her look almost fevered. Perhaps she wasn't doing a good job of hiding anything. Jamie caught Deanna's hand in her own as they went up the stairs, and Deanna didn't think she was imagining the way Jamie's grip had tightened now that they were inside.

Once they reached Deanna's floor, Jamie stopped. Deanna wondered if it would be too soon to invite Jamie back to her apartment—she didn't want to rush things—and hesitated at the door.

"I'm glad you invited me out tonight," Jamie said. "It was really fun."

"Yeah." Deanna hoped that Jamie wouldn't take the relief in her voice the wrong way. She wanted this to be more than one night. "I'm glad you came." Since she hadn't spoken for most of the walk back, her voice was soft and her words caught in her throat as Jamie closed the distance between them.

Jamie's hand was light on Deanna's waist as she drew Deanna closer, and Deanna's eyes dropped to Jamie's mouth as her own mouth parted. She saw a quick flash of white teeth when Jamie grinned, and then Jamie's face dipped close, and their lips brushed. Deanna melted into the kiss, swaying forward when Jamie's grip grew firmer and she deepened the kiss until Deanna's entire focus was on the hot, wet heat of Jamie's mouth. Deanna's eyes closed, and she made a helpless noise of pleasure when Jamie's tongue slid against hers.

Jamie sucked in a breath and then stepped back, giving Deanna's hand one last squeeze. Deanna's lips felt flayed, naked, now that Jamie's were no longer pressed against them.

"Have a good night." Jamie's voice was husky, and color lit her cheeks as she turned and made her way up the stairs. Deanna stayed where she was until she heard the door close on the eighth floor landing, and then, lifting a hand to touch her fingertips to her still-parted mouth, she let herself onto her floor.

Chapter Five |

HER DATE—AN ACTUAL, REAL, OFFICIAL date—with Jamie wasn't for another half an hour. So naturally Deanna had been ready to go for fifteen minutes already. She'd had the day off, and used the excuse to spend a couple of hours at the mall before meeting her friend Max for a quick lunch. She'd been worried about running into Jamie with her handful of bags and in her errand-running jeans, but she'd made it back to her apartment unseen.

Deanna paced the length of her main room a handful of times before she gave up, moved to the couch and dragged her laptop onto the coffee table. She opened Twitter to see what her friends were up to. She was relatively new to the website, having signed up at her employer's request when she'd taken the job with *Wolf's Run* and being given the head moderator handle @denmother, which Deanna found both amusing and appropriate. She'd created her own private account as well, and used that to keep track of her friends and her favorite food trucks. The *Wolf's Run* account was open on her screen, though, so Deanna gave herself a few minutes to scroll through her notifications.

The game was popular enough that she had a hundred or so @ mentions every day. Most of them were friendly despite the occasional griping over an inappropriate post Deanna had to take down. They didn't allow nudity, personal information, threats or hate speech on any of the public message boards, and there were always those who ignored the rules or thought that trolling other members was a classy and entertaining way to spend their time.

Hey @denmother When will WR have a block feature?

Its called #freespeech @denmother DEAL WITH IT

@wolfsrunofficial @denmother loving the new howl system awooooo

Thanks for acting quickly on the post I flagged! @denmother

@denmother Protecting the wolves from trolls one dickwad at a time.

If you keep silencing me @denmother you'll see exactly what I'm capable of. I know what to do with bitches like you. crywolf

Deanna flipped the bird at her computer screen, ignoring the way her heart had stuttered in her chest. Crywolf was one of the least savory aspects of her job. She wasn't sure that he was a "he," though it stood to reason—but he'd begun posting a few months ago, harassing the game players with crudely worded rants about werewolves and the humans who pretended to be them. He seemed to be suffering under the delusion that he actually *was* one. Every time she shut him down he created another account, never using the same username twice, but always ending each post with his signature: crywolf.

He'd kept his anger to *Wolf's Run* forums until now, and seeing crywolf on Twitter was enough to give Deanna a jolt. It wasn't difficult to find any of the game's staff on Twitter—their tweets were featured on the front page of *Wolf's Run*. That he'd moved to another medium was not concerning, exactly, but definitely unpleasant.

Deanna leaned back, pursing her lips as she stared at her computer screen. If crywolf was posting on Twitter, he'd probably shown up again on *Wolf's Run* as well. Her fingers itched as she fought the urge to logon and see what he'd said. It was her day off, though, which meant that, for tonight at least, he was someone else's problem. And she was definitely not going to give him the satisfaction of making her care enough to look at whatever vile thing he was saying this time.

With a determined huff, Deanna closed the lid of her laptop. She probably should report the tweet and the Twitter profile crywolf had created, but she didn't want to spend the few minutes before Jamie arrived focused on him. He wasn't worth that much of her time or attention.

Then again, she considered, if she didn't report him right away she might come back to a deluge of further abuse. Deanna reached again for her laptop, but stopped when Arthur leaped off the couch beside her and made a beeline to the front door with his tail wagging. Deanna glanced at her phone. It was already seven o'clock, and seconds later there was a knock at her door.

"Coming!" she called, and tucked her phone into her purse.

"Hey." Deanna beamed, swinging the door open so that Jamie could step inside.

"Hi." Jamie smiled before she ducked down to rub Arthur's belly—he had instantly dropped to the floor and rolled over for her. Deanna was glad for the momentary distraction. In a pair of slim, olive-colored jeans with a matching tie tucked into a navy blue vest, and a blue-striped dress shirt under a soft-looking gray blazer, Jamie looked so good that Deanna needed a moment to compose herself. The navy and olive made Jamie's skin, peeking out at the collar of her shirt and her wrists, glow a warm, touchable gold. Deanna really, really wanted to touch. The problem was that if she started touching she was pretty sure they wouldn't make it to dinner.

Jamie rose and, as though she had read Deanna's mind, caught Deanna's wrist and drew her close so she could press her lips to Deanna's in a barely-there kiss.

"Ready to go?"

Deanna was ready to stay in. They should stay in. They could stay in, and Deanna could order pizza and then they wouldn't have to leave, ever. She had plenty of food in her fridge so, really, they wouldn't have to leave for at least three days. "Yeah, sure," she agreed.

Jamie gave Arthur one last pat, and Deanna picked up her keys and they left.

The restaurant Jamie had picked was Ethiopian, and Deanna had never had Ethiopian food. It was in a house, with all the rooms converted into dining areas, so when they were shown to their table on the second floor, tucked into a small corner by the window of what Deanna was pretty sure used to be part of the bedroom, she couldn't help but be utterly charmed.

Deanna was further charmed when Jamie suggested they opt for a bottle of wine. From the few encounters they'd had, Deanna knew Jamie preferred beer. Appreciating the gesture, Deanna chose a pleasant bottle of Sauvignon Blanc.

Jamie gave an appreciative hum as she tasted the wine, and in doing so gave Deanna all sorts of R-rated thoughts about what she could do that Jamie would appreciate. Trying to stay on course, Deanna turned her attention to the menu, hoping to find something she'd recognize. She wasn't adventurous with her restaurant choices, generally preferring to stick to her tried and true favorites, but she'd been so pleased at the idea of a real date with Jamie that she'd accepted the offer of Ethiopian without question.

"A lot of these appetizers are good," Jamie said, interrupting Deanna's perusal of her options. "Back with my pa—" she broke off, face reddening as Deanna raised a quizzical eyebrow. "Back with my, er, parents," Jamie continued, rubbing a hand over her mouth, "we'd share a few of them. Sound good?"

"Sure." Deanna wasn't sure what had thrown Jamie, but didn't plan to ask. Jamie's family was her own business, and Deanna certainly wasn't one to pry. Well, not on a first date, anyway. Now a second date, on the other hand…

Not that Deanna was thinking so far into the future. That would be ridiculous. Really, she'd barely met Jamie. Hardly knew a thing about her. They were practically strangers. It was only that Deanna's crush seemed to be growing exponentially with every minor interaction. She'd gotten a text from Jamie yesterday about dinner and had spent the next hour of work grinning blissfully at her computer screen, barely registering what she was doing as she'd cleared her queue.

It helped to know that Jamie seemed to be as infatuated as Deanna was. Well, maybe not *as* infatuated, but close. The kiss they'd shared after the walk home from trivia night was scorching enough that Deanna didn't doubt Jamie's attraction to her.

The one thing she didn't want to do, though, was U-Haul it. She'd seen enough of her friends embark on that disastrous venture that she was properly in camp take-it-slow. And not *too slowly*, she amended, watching Jamie rattle off an order to their server without consulting the menu. Was everyone this sexy when they ordered confidently, or was Deanna just wearing Jamie goggles?

"Do you have a big family, then?" Deanna asked once the server had vanished, having entirely forgotten her determination not to pry.

"No, it's really just me." Jamie gave an elegant shrug. "My parents are back east, and I never had any siblings."

"Oh." Deanna frowned, not a little confused. "I just thought—I mean, you ordered like eight different things and there's only the two of us…"

Jamie looked blankly at Deanna before something clicked into place and she coughed. "Uh, yeah. No, sorry. I have a big… extended family." She gave a sheepish shrug. "I'm used to ordering for all of us."

Deanna laughed. "It's no problem. I'm more than happy to eat leftovers for lunch. And I know what it's like to have a large extended family."

"Yeah?"

"Oh, yeah." Deanna launched into a story of her last family reunion, where her Aunt Leita had made an entire bowl of sangria vanish and then informed a teenaged Deanna and her brother about the various illegal substances they ought to try, before Deanna's horrified father had put a stop to what Deanna had found to be a very educational speech.

Jamie retaliated with a story about her Uncle Trevor who'd instigated a board game night—what she and her cousins back home had taken to referring to as "bored game" night—and that they actually drew straws to determine which of them would have to go every month.

Deanna was already on her third plate of food before she realized how much she was enjoying her meal. To be fair, it was hard not to like fried cheese. She'd been so distracted watching Jamie talk that she'd hardly noticed Jamie filling her plate for her. While Deanna was a wildly expressive talker, all hands and animated features, Jamie was quieter and more composed in her storytelling. So Deanna tracked every gentle movement and small smile and was delighted when, after Deanna made a rather unfortunate comparison between their landlord and a gopher, Jamie threw back her head and laughed until there were tears in her eyes.

If Jamie did bring up a U-Haul, Deanna was so in. Not that she'd need an actual U-Haul to move up one floor, anyway.

At the end of the meal, Deanna had been more than ready to find out what an Ethiopian dessert would taste like; but Jamie surprised her with the offer to go back to her place for something sweet.

She'd actually said that, "something sweet," and while Deanna had been ninety-eight percent sure that Jamie was being perfectly earnest, there was the slightest curve to her wide mouth that made Deanna take a large gulp of water before she could answer with any composure.

As they headed back toward the apartment building, Deanna pulled out her phone to check the time and couldn't muffle the groan of annoyance as she saw the ridiculous number of notifications she had.

"What's wrong?" Jamie laid a hand on the small of Deanna's back, concern tugging at her features.

"It's nothing—just a work thing." When Jamie raised an expectant eyebrow, Deanna sighed and elaborated, not wanting to allow crywolf into her date night. But if she brushed it off, Jamie might bring it up again later. Better to just get it over with. "You might have heard that guys on the Internet can be assholes? *Wolf's Run* has its own particular jackoff called crywolf, who seems to have nothing better to do than spam our members, message boards, and now my official Twitter account with bizarrely worded threats." Deanna brought up the most recent one and read: "'My big teeth are waiting @denmother. Do you taste as sweet as you look?'" The words left a bad taste in Deanna's mouth.

"Shit." Jamie's arm curled around Deanna's waist, drawing her in until Jamie's hip pressed against her side. Deanna considered this new development before sending an ironic mental thank you to crywolf. She could dig this whole "protective girlfriend" thing. Not that Jamie was her girlfriend. Yet.

"Doesn't that worry you?" Jamie asked.

Deanna shrugged against Jamie's side. "It's the Internet. People leave their manners in the real world."

"Still." Deanna could hear the frown in Jamie's voice.

"It's okay, honestly. I've had worse. It just comes with the territory. I'm sure you get some weird crap doing fieldwork for your research."

"Nothing like that." Jamie shook her head but let the matter drop as they reached their building.

Wanting to take Arthur for a short walk, Deanna begged to postpone their date for fifteen minutes. Jamie readily agreed, and on the seventh floor Deanna gave in to the urge she'd been fighting all night and drew Jamie down for a kiss that echoed their first—slick and wet and with the slightest hint of tongue. When she pulled back, Jamie's skin was flushed, and Deanna couldn't help but nip lightly at Jamie's swollen bottom lip. Jamie's indrawn breath made things low in Deanna's body clench, and with a breathless laugh she darted toward her door, hoping that Arthur would make their trip outside a quick one.

When Deanna let Arthur back into their apartment—ignoring his heavy doggy sigh at being left alone again—she dropped off her coat as well. It seemed a bit silly to bring her purse and shoes when she was only going one floor up, but she was wearing a dress again and they never had pockets. Deanna wasn't going to leave her phone behind or her front door unlocked. Noting that her self-imposed deadline of fifteen minutes was almost up, she ran her comb through her hair. No matter what she tried, the humidity made it a frizzy mess by the end of the night. She dabbed a bit more color onto her lips, hoping to balance the rosy cheeks that the wine and anticipation had given her, and finished with a spritz of her favorite perfume.

Giving herself a critical once-over in the mirror, Deanna decided she looked gorgeous. Her hair would frizz in a matter of minutes, but she ignored that and turned on her heel to make her way upstairs as nerves danced in the pit of her stomach.

Jamie had thoughtfully left her own front door slightly ajar, and Deanna stepped through with a light knock just in case Jamie, like Deanna, was also indulging in a last minute primp.

"Welcome back to my—what did Nathan call it last time—'humble abode'?" Jamie called from the kitchen where she stood behind the counter opening a bottle of wine.

As Deanna made her way across the living room to join her, the apartment echoed with the sharp pop of bubbly being opened, and she couldn't help the coo of pleasure the sound elicited.

"You really didn't need to go to all this effort," she said as she slid onto one of the bar stools.

"What effort? You think I don't always have some Prosecco on hand?" Jamie arched an eyebrow, and the haughty curve of it drew the breath from Deanna's lungs. She gripped the edge of the stool with both hands to stop herself from squirming, suddenly feeling as if her skin was stretched hot and tight.

Deanna licked her lips. "I…"

"Only teasing," Jamie said with a wink, crossing the room to hand Deanna a flute of the pink bubbly. "I actually had to go pick up a couple of these." She raised her own glass and tapped it lightly against Deanna's.

Deanna knew she was probably as pink as the wine and chose to tilt the glass back and take a sip instead of answering. The bubbles hit her tongue, and she closed her eyes with a murmur of delight. She felt giddy enough without the added wine, but couldn't resist taking another mouthful and rolling it around with her tongue. Since a bottle of wine was more than she would usually drink in one sitting, and anything sparkling didn't stay sparkling overnight, Deanna rarely had the chance to indulge. And Jamie, intentionally or not, had picked a delicious bottle.

"I'm glad you did." Expression serious, Deanna looked over the top of her glass at Jamie. "I have a firm policy against sleeping with anyone who doesn't own proper champagne flutes."

Jamie's eyes widened, and she choked on her mouthful of wine. Deanna laughed so hard that she had to set her glass down. It took Jamie a minute to recover, and Deanna was still giggling helplessly when Jamie moved toward her.

Deanna swallowed her laughter as Jamie closed in. The other woman had taken off her jacket and vest, removed her tie and rolled the sleeves of her dress shirt up her forearms. When Deanna twisted around on the stool to keep Jamie in sight, Jamie bracketed her, and it took Deanna a second to drag her eyes away from those bare forearms, with their light dusting of soft hair. Deanna had leaned back as Jamie moved closer, and the edge of the counter dug into her back as she tried to take a deep breath and slow the pounding of her heart. She could feel the heat of Jamie's arms against her own, though Jamie had been careful to not quite touch. That almost-contact was torture, and when Deanna's eyes finally got past the hollow of Jamie's throat, her golden skin framed so deliciously by the crisp white collar, Deanna knew it had been on purpose.

The breath she'd taken escaped in a sudden rush, and Jamie pressed in; Deanna's thighs parted automatically until Jamie stood between them. The rasp of denim against the bare skin of her legs where her dress had ridden up made Deanna shiver, and Jamie's whiskey-colored eyes darkened in response.

"Should we leave dessert for after?" Jamie pushed closer, her words ghosting against Deanna's parted lips.

It took Deanna a moment to answer, the tightness in her throat making her response breathier than she'd intended. "Please."

Jamie's teeth flashed in a grin, and Deanna had a second to marvel at how positively wolfish those white teeth made her look before Jamie's hands were in her hair and she was dragging Deanna's head back to bite at the column of her exposed neck.

Deanna's legs wrapped around Jamie and pulled her closer; her hips jerked when Jamie's tongue laved the mark her teeth had left. Jamie's body gave an answering roll and Deanna groaned as Jamie's lips found her own.

Jamie pulled her hands free from Deanna's curls, gripped the back of her thighs and pulled her up off the stool. Deanna squeaked as she locked her arms around Jamie's neck, afraid she'd fall.

"Let me down! I can walk, I can walk," she protested, laughing. Jamie was muscular but she wasn't that much bigger than Deanna, and Deanna really didn't want Jamie to strain any muscles before they got to the important part of the evening. Not that she wasn't enjoying the display of strength; it was turning Deanna's insides into jelly.

"No," Jamie growled against the sensitive skin of Jamie's throat, and Deanna's next protest died on her lips.

Deanna tried to pay attention as they moved down the hallway, but she didn't catch more than a flash of the dove-gray walls before Jamie shoved open the door to her bedroom. She had Deanna pressed back against the soft give of a mattress before she could do more than blink. Deanna was still adjusting to lying flat when Jamie slid a hand between her legs and cupped the center of her.

Deanna made a strangled noise and arched into the touch; her hands clutched the bed sheets when Jamie increased the pressure, moving the base of her palm in steady, maddening circles against Deanna's clit. Deanna's hips rose to meet the touch as Jamie bowed, head dipping to suck a bruise into the heaving flesh of Deanna's breast where it rose over the top of her dress.

The aching pain was enough to send Deanna over the edge, and with a bitten-off curse she came, gushing wet and hot into Jamie's hand. Jamie didn't give her a moment to recover before she slipped her fingers under the soaked fabric of Deanna's panties and into Deanna.

Deanna tore her hands free of the sheets to yank desperately at Jamie's shirt, needing to feel Jamie's skin against her own, as Jamie found the spot inside her that had Deanna's eyes fluttering closed and her nails digging ruthlessly into Jamie's back.

"Please, just let me—" Deanna struggled to pull in enough air as Jamie twisted two fingers into her and Deanna could have sworn she saw stars. "Just—fuck!" She convulsed around Jamie and felt the other woman grin widely against her skin. As the last waves of pleasure shuddered through her, Deanna fell lax against the bed with her hands sliding bonelessly off a still-very-much-clothed Jamie and realized that she, too, was still fully dressed.

Jamie leaned back, bringing her slick fingers to her mouth. Deanna made a soft noise of frustration and pushed herself up onto her elbows; her legs were still weak and trembling.

"Clothes. Off. Now," she demanded.

"So impatient," Jamie remarked with no small amount of smugness.

"Says the woman who wouldn't even let me have dessert—or finish my glass of wine."

Deanna watched with half-lidded eyes as Jamie unbuttoned her shirt. In a moment Deanna would sit up and pull her dress fully off, but for now she was more than happy to lie back and watch Jamie's skin appear inch by inch as she worked her way down the buttons.

Jamie unclasped her simple white bra in the front and dropped it before she was forced to move off the bed and stand to work her tight jeans down her legs. The thought of all that dusky skin against her own forced Deanna into action, and she sat up to yank her dress free, then shoved it somewhere off the bed. Her bra and panties followed moments later. Naked and completely unashamed, Deanna moved forward on her knees until she was at the edge of the bed, where she hooked her fingers into the wide band of Jamie's underwear as she finally kicked her way free of her pants.

Jamie's hands came to push her underwear down, but Deanna caught her fingers and stopped her, leaning in to lick quick and catlike at Jamie's hardened nipple. Jamie's fingers stilled, her eyes fell shut and color rose high on her cheeks as Deanna pulled Jamie closer until the heat of her radiated against the bare skin of Deanna's front.

Deanna drew Jamie's nipple into her mouth; her tongue teased the stiff flesh until Jamie made a high, helpless sound in her throat. Deanna slid her hands around Jamie's sides, dipped under the band of her underwear and gripped her ass with both hands as she tried to work more of Jamie's hot flesh into her mouth. Jamie writhed against her; her hands rested lightly on Deanna's shoulders as Deanna slid her fingers into the cleft of Jamie's ass and then lower.

Because of the angle, Deanna couldn't do more than slide the pad of her finger over Jamie's slick opening, and Jamie's angry mewl of frustration made everything in Deanna's body clench. She could feel how damp she still was between her own legs; her thighs were wet with arousal and orgasm, and after another teasing stroke over Jamie she relented. Pushing Jamie's underwear down, she released Jamie's breast and scooted back on the bed so Jamie could join her.

Jamie tried to push Deanna into the mattress, but Deanna wriggled free. Jamie let Deanna shove her back. Since Jamie had already displayed in the living room that she was more than strong enough to move Deanna where she wanted her, Deanna was pleased that she yielded.

A red bruise was already blooming around Jamie's nipple, and Deanna dropped a light kiss over the abused flesh, though she couldn't deny how the thought of having marked Jamie, and over such a sensitive place—so that whenever her shirt or bra scraped over the tender skin she'd think of Deanna—thrilled her.

"Deanna."

She caught Jamie's desperate gaze. Jamie had raked a hand through her carefully styled hair, and it fell in disarray around her face. Unlike Deanna, Jamie always appeared completely put together. Even in jeans and a T-shirt she expressed an air of total confidence and comfort. Her disheveled hair, even more than her nakedness, sharpened Deanna's desire until she could feel the bite of it like a physical pain.

Careful to be gentle despite the storm that raged within her, Deanna pressed a hand to Jamie's belly, urging her to lie flat. When Jamie complied, Deanna moved down Jamie's body, dropping light kisses down her stomach until she reached the dark thatch of hair between her legs.

Jamie quivered under Deanna's lips but followed Deanna's wordless instruction, keeping herself still as Deanna shouldered her legs apart and settled comfortably between them. With her cheek pressed against Jamie's thigh, Deanna could see the rapid rise and fall of Jamie's breathing and the flush that spilled over her cheeks to her throat and spread over the thin skin of her chest. Deanna nuzzled against the raised mound of Jamie's pubis; the soft hair curled against her face as she breathed in the scent of Jamie's arousal.

Unlike Deanna, Jamie's slickness was gathered at the center of her, and Deanna used gentle fingers to part her folds. She was wet and pink, a vivid contrast to the darkness of her hair, and Deanna paused with her teeth sunk into her own bottom lip as she drank in the sight before her: as intoxicating—no, more so than the pink Prosecco.

Jamie's hips gave an unconscious twitch and a whine of frustration rose in her throat. Deanna breathed out a soft laugh before she pressed a wet, open-mouthed kiss to Jamie's swollen clit. Jamie froze, her thighs tense around Deanna as Deanna used the flat of her tongue to glide lightly over that responsive bundle of nerves. She stroked once, twice, movements slow enough to be agonizing for both of them before she sucked Jamie into her mouth. She kept up the rhythm, slow and insistent, echoing her earlier pull of Jamie's breast.

Jamie's hand came down, pushed against the back of Deanna's head as she tried to increase the pressure—but, instead of complying, Deanna stopped. Lifting her face, parted lips glistening, she gave her head a single shake as she met Jamie's eyes, her pupils blown wide and blurry. With a dissatisfied whimper, Jamie dropped her hand, flattening it against the mattress. Only when Deanna was sure Jamie wouldn't move did she bring her lips back down to rub over Jamie's clit, touch even lighter than her tongue had been.

"Deanna." Jamie's voice was a broken plea; her legs shook as she fought to hold herself still and not thrust up into Deanna's mouth. Deanna brought a hand down from Jamie's waist and pressed it between her own legs, rocking against her fingers as she finally took pity on Jamie and tongued at her in earnest.

Jamie lifted off the bed at Deanna's increased movements; her ragged breathing filled the room as Deanna pushed them both closer to orgasm. With a hard suck at Jamie's clit and the slightest graze of teeth, Jamie cried out and shook against Deanna; her hand grabbed Deanna's hair. Deanna moaned in approval against Jamie's wet heat before pulling her mouth away to sink her teeth bruisingly into the soft flesh of Jamie's trembling thigh as she rode her own hand to another shattering orgasm.

AFTERWARD, JAMIE ROSE TO PULL on new underwear and a tank top, but Deanna stayed happily naked in Jamie's bed, watching with the quiet contentment of a cat as Jamie returned with the neglected Prosecco and a small plate of baklava. Deanna sat up to take the glass Jamie offered, not bothering to cover herself. The wine was still pleasantly cool.

Deanna still felt flushed and warm with the afterglow, but as Jamie settled back against the headboard Deanna snuggled close beside her.

47

Jamie was radiating even more heat than Deanna; Deanna could have sworn she could feel it sinking into her bones like a hot bath, but the touch of the cool wine against her lips was a soothing counterpoint to her overstimulated nerves.

Though Deanna was usually unable to stop herself from saying every other thought that came into her head, post-orgasm Deanna was more than happy to indulge in silence. Jamie seemed equally content to say nothing. Sipping her wine, she stroked a slow hand over Deanna's hair, but not through it, because the curls were hopelessly tangled. Deanna had a nibble of baklava but couldn't bring herself to go through the effort of sitting up to eat more, choosing instead to lick the sticky honey from her fingers and then wrap her arm around Jamie's stomach.

"Do you want to stay the night?" When Jamie did break the silence, Deanna realized that she'd been half-dozing with her champagne flute propped against Jamie's hip.

"Mmm, I shouldn't." Reluctantly, Deanna pushed herself up until she was sitting. "Thank you for offering, but Arthur worries. And I know you have an early class."

The idea of staying was enticing, but Deanna had no intention of overstaying her welcome and letting this relationship fizzle out before it had a chance to become something. Not that she suspected that was likely, not after the incredible sex they'd just had, but she didn't want to risk it. Because Deanna definitely wanted to see Jamie again—and oh, god, she wanted to fuck Jamie again.

"If you're sure," Jamie said, watching as Deanna pulled her dress over her shoulders. She didn't bother with her panties or her bra. After all, she was only going one floor down, and they'd fit easily enough in her purse.

"I'm sure," Deanna confirmed and kissed Jamie. Jamie's hands ran up Deanna's forearms and gave a quick squeeze as Deanna pulled back. "Thank you for the delightful evening," she said, lingering in the doorway of the bedroom to appreciate the image of Jamie sprawled and sated on the bed.

"It was my pleasure." Jamie's lips quirked in a smirk that had Deanna questioning whether she ought to crawl back into the bed and—no, best not. She let herself drag her gaze down Jamie's body one last time. Her brow furrowed when she noticed that the bruise she'd carefully dug into Jamie's thigh with her teeth as she'd come the final time hadn't turned out to be much of a bruise at all. In fact, there wasn't a trace of Deanna's teeth left against the delicate skin of Jamie's inner thigh.

Dismissing her disappointment with a small shake of her head—she'd just have to try harder, and she was fairly certain Jamie wouldn't mind—Deanna blew a cheeky kiss to Jamie and went back to her apartment.

Chapter Six |

HAVING JAMIE ONE FLOOR ABOVE her was excruciating. Deanna came to this conclusion three days after their date. She hadn't seen Jamie since that night, but knowing that her lover—and what a thrill it was to use the word *lover*, even if it was only in her head—was at any moment walking across the floor above Deanna was enough to drive her crazy.

The floors were thick enough that Deanna couldn't actually hear Jamie move about, but since they'd been texting nearly nonstop since the morning after they'd had sex, Deanna knew when Jamie was home. They'd tried to schedule a second date, but one of Deanna's coworkers had come down with a nasty case of the flu so Deanna had agreed to pick up a couple of extra shifts. Naturally, those shifts were the night ones.

So, while Jamie might have the evening off, Deanna didn't.

With a heavy sigh, and well aware of how melodramatic she was being, Deanna pulled her focus back to the computer screen in front of her. She had four more hours left and then she could go to bed. She could handle four more hours without texting Jamie and inviting herself upstairs.

Deanna rolled her shoulders back and clicked on the next item in her queue. On the desk beside her, the screen of her phone lit up with an incoming text. Deanna abandoned her queue and grabbed the phone. Though reserved in person, Deanna had learned that Jamie could be nearly chatty over text.

Okay I know you're working and I'm not supposed to be distracting you. And I'm also supposed to be working and not getting distracted. But the interview I'm transcribing is REALLY BORING.

Deanna grinned, fingers flying over the touchpad, as she replied. **One of us needs to have self-control, here. Pretty sure you called dibs on that one.**

Jamie's response came seconds later. **I don't remember calling dibs on self-control?**

You called it by default by being the responsible one.

??????

Master's degree + fancy adult apartment + owns a real mattress with a box spring = responsible.

Jamie's reply made Deanna laugh out loud. **And you told me you were bad at math.**

Deanna's computer pinged with an incoming flag, and Deanna rubbed a hand guiltily over her mouth. She really did need to be working.

All right, I'll be the responsible one & get back to work. I'll message you on my break!

I'll be waiting.

Deanna was helpless against the giddy flutter in her chest and had to force herself to put her phone back onto the desk, even going so far as to turn it face down so she wouldn't get distracted again by an incoming text. As she turned back to her computer, she pressed a hand to her heated cheeks and willed herself to pay attention to her job.

Two hours later Deanna stood, informed of her fifteen-minute break by the chime of her phone. She rolled her neck from side to side and stretched out her arms before picking up her phone and idly wandering into the kitchen. Sitting for too long was as bad as smoking—or so she'd read somewhere—and Deanna tried to make sure that she moved on her breaks.

She had a string of texts from Jamie, and couldn't resist the urge to skip over to the bowl of apples on the small counter. Deanna chose the reddest one and bit down as she began to scroll through Jamie's messages.

I've given up on transcribing for the night. I'm going to watch a movie.

I went with *Sweet Home Alabama*. It's not terrible. It would be better if I had someone to cuddle with, though ☹

(All right. I feel bad about that last text. You're working and I shouldn't be guilting you.)

This movie is in fact terrible. I'm switching to *Wedding Crashers*.

This movie is also not good. This text was accompanied by a picture of Jamie's face with her wide mouth turned down in an adorable pout. Deanna checked the timestamp—it had been sent three minutes ago. She began to type a reply.

I have ten minutes.

Technically, Deanna had thirteen, but she figured it would take Jamie at least three to read the text and get down the stairs. Taking another bite of her apple, she tossed her phone on the armchair and was about to check her hair in the bathroom mirror when there was a knock at the door.

Arthur scrabbled up from his bed and gave a happy bark. Sure it couldn't be Jamie already—maybe Heather needed something?—Deanna strode to the door, then shoved Arthur out of the way to look through the peephole.

It *was* Jamie, and, with a puzzled smile, Deanna opened the door to let her in.

"Were you already on your way down?" she joked, as Jamie gave Arthur a quick rub. Jamie didn't look like someone who'd just raced down two hallways and a flight of stairs. Deanna would have been at least a little breathless, but Jamie didn't have a hair out of place.

"I was in the neighborhood." Jamie straightened gracefully and gave Deanna a cheeky grin before she closed the door behind her and moved easily into the room. Jamie wore her customary jeans, black this time, and an equally black V-neck shirt that made it nearly impossible for Deanna to pull her eyes away from the tantalizing hollow of Jamie's throat. Screw her apple. She wanted to take a bite out of Jamie's collarbone.

As though Jamie could read Deanna's mind, or hear the way her pulse had sped up, Jamie stepped closer, crowding into Deanna's space. Deanna's mouth parted, and, when Jamie pressed a searing kiss to Deanna's lips, the apple fell with a thud that Deanna barely heard, too busy grabbing fistfuls of Jamie's T-shirt and returning the kiss with a heated enthusiasm that left them both breathless.

"Ten minutes, less." Deanna reminded as they stumbled to Deanna's couch; neither of them was willing to take their hands or mouths off each other. Jamie didn't waste time responding, merely tugged them both to the cushions and buried her hands in Deanna's hair. Deanna pressed forward to kiss Jamie again, Jamie's kiss-swollen mouth irresistible, but Jamie held her back and Deanna made a wounded noise of protest.

"Just let me look at you," Jamie urged. She smoothed her fingers through Deanna's hair, her movements soft and gentle. Deanna settled, running her own hands up Jamie's muscular forearms.

"Is it too soon to say I missed you?" Deanna asked, too happy to have Jamie in her apartment to feel embarrassed.

Jamie shook her head. Her warm brown eyes never left Deanna's. "I missed you too. I want to see you again."

Deanna raised a teasing eyebrow. "You're seeing me now."

"Dinner," Jamie clarified. "Or lunch. Breakfast. Coffee."

"Well, I *was* having a snack," Deanna nodded to the discarded apple that Arthur was giving a cautious lick.

"Are you working tomorrow? Can we go out? Let me take you out."

Jamie had slid her hands down from Deanna's hair, and her thumbs rubbed soothing circles into the muscles of Deanna's neck. It took Deanna a moment to find the answer to Jamie's question. Her brain insisted that there was no need to think about work when she could be thinking about what else Jamie could do with those clever fingers. "Um. I start at three. We can do lunch."

"Good." Jamie gave Deanna a soft kiss that made every bone in Deanna's body melt until she swayed into Jamie's arms. "What about the day after that?"

"Trivia," Deanna murmured, her eyes dropping back to that enticing triangle of skin at Jamie's throat.

"I like trivia."

"You should come." Deanna licked her lips. "The day after that's my day off." They could go out, visit an art gallery, wander through downtown. Deanna could hold Jamie's hand and listen to Jamie talk about her thesis. They could have a nice dinner. Or they could stay in.

"All right. I call dibs." Jamie's teeth flashed in her wide smile, and she kissed Deanna quickly and fiercely. Then, with her customary fluid grace, she extracted herself and before Deanna had recovered from the kiss was at the door. "Time's up." She gave Arthur a rub on his belly and slipped out with a jaunty wave.

Deanna groaned and flopped back against the cushions. Time to get back to work.

Chapter Seven |

Occasionally, Deanna liked to grab Arthur and her laptop and go outside for a change of scenery. The rain had finally eased off as the flowers started blooming—whoever had introduced cherry trees to North America had Deanna's eternal gratitude—and Deanna was happy to leave her raincoat behind, opting instead for a light spring jacket. Arthur was beside himself as they moved down the block in the warm sun, though he was too well-trained to pull on the leash as they walked toward another of Vancouver's many public parks.

Deanna stopped at a coffee shop, popping in to grab a vanilla latte with whipped cream, before they settled at one of the picnic benches strewn about the park. On a weekday at three the place was as close to deserted as it ever was on a sunny afternoon. There was a scattering of mothers or nannies with young children and the occasional elderly couple out for a stroll, but by and large she and Arthur had the place to themselves.

Putting her bag and coffee on the table, Deanna turned to Arthur and fixed him with a beady eye. "If I let you off the leash you have to stay close to me. None of this running into the forest, call of the wild bullshit, you hear me?"

Arthur gave a soft whine; his gaze darted past her to fix on a chittering squirrel at the base of a nearby tree.

"Hey, buddy, I'm talking to you."

With obvious reluctance, he pulled his attention back to her and gave a hopeful wag of his tail. Deanna narrowed her eyes, but unclipped his leash. Arthur didn't bother to wait a minute for politeness's sake, but took off like a shot toward the squirrel, who abruptly swallowed its teasing and scurried up the trunk of a tree. Arthur plunked his butt down and settled in to wait.

With half an ear out for the jangle of his collar, in case Arthur went on the move again, Deanna pulled her computer out of her bag and set up, plugging in her mobile Internet stick so she could connect to the *Wolf's Run* site.

For a couple of hours she worked steadily, clearing her queue of messages and posts that had been flagged or reported and dealing with only one slightly tricky issue, in which the alleged behavior had occurred off-site and now both parties were unhappy that the other remained active. Since nothing else popped up that required her attention, and her shift was almost up, Deanna pulled out her phone and opened the *Wolf's Run* app.

She had an official account on *Wolf's Run*, but when Deanna applied for the job she'd also downloaded the app and set up a profile to see what the game was all about. She'd enjoyed playing for the couple of weeks before she'd heard back from the administrative team, and though she hadn't been very active on the message boards, she'd made a couple of posts. Staff weren't discouraged from playing the game, but they were cautioned about keeping their private accounts private, and of course restricted from anything that could be seen as cheating or using their behind-the-scenes knowledge to unfair advantage. Because of that, Deanna had made a point of not getting involved with the role-playing aspect of it, avoided the forums and storyboards once she'd been hired and did nothing that could directly affect the plot. But she was a sucker for the real-world interaction of claiming territory for her pack and so, knowing she was currently in a hotly contested area, she logged in to make her claim for the Hollow Cave Pack.

Logging in brought her automatically to her profile, and Deanna spent a moment admiring the werewolf avatar she'd created. The website offered an impressive array of selections and customizations, and Deanna had created a seven foot-tall wolfman—well, wolflady—with pale gray markings, royal blue eyes and a broadsword slung over her back. It might have been overkill to include the sword, but Deanna had wanted the most badass lady werewolf possible. The site encouraged users to upload pictures of themselves for their character's human appearance, and an important piece of the game's werewolf lore was that when a werewolf transformed from human into wolfman, his eyes stayed the same color. If you uploaded your own picture, the computer would recognize your eye color and transmit that to your avatar. It was a pretty neat feature, but since Deanna was keeping her private account private, she hadn't taken advantage of it; hence her avatar had blue eyes instead of green. Even without Deanna's eyes, she thought her character looked pretty cool.

As she moved her thumb to claim the territory at her current location, a notification informed her that she had a new private message (or a howl, as they were called in the game).

Since Deanna didn't interact with any other users on this account, she was surprised. She brought the message up.

Hey D. Betchya didn't think I could find you here. Too bad that REAL WOLVES are great trackers. Be a good den mommy and take down the site. Or I'll keep tracking. crywolf

Deanna wasn't sure how long she stared at the text. Her fingers were numb where she clutched her phone; her chest was tight with a sensation she refused to recognize as panic. It wasn't until Arthur came over and dropped his head onto her thigh that Deanna snapped out of it. She set her phone carefully on the table, though she was tempted to fling it as far away from her as she could, and took a deep breath.

Her shift wasn't over yet. She still had a few minutes left, but, since her queue was empty of any issues that needed resolving, Deanna just sat there and stared at the screen. She should log back on to her private account and submit an abuse report about crywolf and the account he'd used to send the message, but she couldn't look at it again. Not right now.

When the clock showed five, Deanna logged out of her moderator account and shut her laptop, tucking it into her bag before she hooked Arthur onto his leash. For once he didn't try to linger as they left the park, but stuck close by her side as they made their way home.

She should stop at the grocery store—Deanna had told Jamie that she would make her dinner—but she couldn't bring herself to leave Arthur tied up outside while she shopped. It wasn't as though crywolf was actually *watching* her, but because he'd found her private account when there was no clear connection between that one and her moderator account Deanna was more uneasy than she cared to admit.

Once they were inside, Deanna was unable to sit still. Though she'd just done it last week, she went through each cupboard in the kitchen, pulled out the contents and wiped down the shelves. She'd hoped the mindless task would distract her, but she couldn't shake the sensation of being watched.

"It's silly," she said to Arthur as he wandered into the kitchen. On her knees on the counter, Deanna clutched precariously at the top of the farthest cupboard as she leaned in to get at the back corner. "I'm overreacting."

Arthur put his head on his paws, in what Deanna took to be a sympathetic gesture.

Someone knocked on the front door, and Deanna nearly jumped out of her skin. Her heart pounded in her chest, and it wasn't until Arthur gave a joyous woof that she realized it had to be Jamie. She eased herself off the counter and hurried across the room. Though Arthur was already wriggling beside the door, Deanna still checked the peephole.

Jamie had a small bouquet of flowers, but instead of handing them to Deanna so that she could pet Arthur, Jamie looked at Deanna.

"Are you all right?"

Deanna nodded. Arthur, maybe sensing that the adults needed to talk, settled into his dog bed.

"I got another message at work today. From crywolf," Deanna explained wearily. "Except it wasn't really *at* work; it was on my personal *Wolf's Run* account, which isn't public knowledge."

Jamie had moved into the apartment, and now pulled Deanna into a hard hug. Deanna buried her face in Jamie's neck and clutched at her. Deanna was embarrassed when tears began to prick at her eyes.

"It's okay," Jamie soothed. Her hand, the one that wasn't still holding the paper-wrapped bouquet, gently rubbed Deanna's back.

Jamie's sweater was soft against Deanna's bare arms and Deanna inhaled the warm scent of Jamie's cologne. For the first time since she'd seen crywolf's message, Deanna felt safe.

"I didn't get groceries," Deanna mumbled against Jamie's skin. "It's kinda chickenshit, I—"

"Hey." Jamie cut her off. "Don't beat yourself up. It's okay to feel scared after something like that."

Deanna gave a watery laugh and stepped back to wipe away the tears. "Thanks. And I know. But." She shrugged. "It's not like he said anything new."

"Can I see the message?"

Deanna nodded and picked up her phone from the coffee table. She pulled up the message before passing it to Jamie, who traded her for the flowers. "It's the same vague and delusional crap."

Jamie's lips thinned as she read the text. "He calls you 'D,'" she said finally, putting the phone down. "That's not a vague threat."

"'D' for 'denmother,' I'm sure." Deanna unwrapped the flowers, a bundle of lilac-colored hyacinths, and arranged them in a glass vase.

"Or 'D' for Deanna," Jamie said darkly.

"Now who's overreacting?" Deanna teased. The sensation of being watched had vanished, and, with Jamie's solid and reassuring presence in the room, Deanna felt even sillier about her reluctance to shop on her way home. "I'm sorry about dinner, though."

"Your famous spaghetti Bolognese can wait." Jamie came into the kitchen behind Deanna and wrapped her arms around her. "What did you do to your cupboards? No, never mind. I don't want to know." She shook her head. "Why don't you run yourself a hot bath? I'll pour you a glass of wine, put your kitchen back together, and then we can order pizza."

"Yeah?" Deanna perked up.

"Yeah," Jamie confirmed. "And you can make me watch a couple episodes of one of your bad sci-fi shows. We'll have a marathon night."

A hot bath and a glass of wine sounded wonderful. "Okay. But *Battlestar Galactica* isn't 'bad sci-fi.' It's amazing."

Wisely, Jamie didn't argue.

As THE CREDITS RAN ON their third episode, Deanna knew she should probably let Jamie go back upstairs. It was a weekday, so she'd have class in the morning. Still, instead of suggesting Jamie leave, she snuggled closer to her warm, solid body.

Jamie shut off the TV and the DVD player. Since they'd closed the heavy blinds before starting the show, the only light came from the small lamp behind the couch. And since the bed was much more comfortable than the couch to cuddle on, Deanna had pulled it out when Jamie went for the pizza, so now she and Jamie lay tangled in the sheets in her barely-lit apartment.

Deanna had emerged from her bath with her skin flushed pink from the heat and the glass of wine Jamie had handed her. She'd put on her favorite nightgown. If they were in for the night, Deanna saw no reason not to be in pjs.

Though she'd spent the last episode with her bare leg tucked between Jamie's jean-clad ones, it wasn't until Jamie turned off the screen, making

Deanna's small apartment that much darker, that Deanna felt the first twist of desire. She'd enjoyed their cuddling, taking simple, human pleasure in the warm body of another person tucked close beside her. But even when Jamie had brushed her fingers over the back of Deanna's neck, a spot that usually pushed all of Deanna's buttons, Deanna had felt only a pleasant curl of warmth.

She slid her leg farther between Jamie's, wondering if the feeling would continue to build or if the events and emotions of the day had taken too much of a toll. Jamie stilled, her hand frozen where it had been slowly stroking Deanna's hair, and when Deanna pressed her thigh higher Jamie took a quick, indrawn breath.

The sound was enough to make Deanna aware of the dampness between her legs and she twisted, so that instead of being beside Jamie she was on top of her.

In the darkness, Jamie's eyes were nearly black. Her lips parted as Deanna rubbed the top of her thigh against Jamie through her jeans. Jamie reached for Deanna, but she just shook her head, and with a groan of frustration, Jamie dropped her hands back to the bed.

Jamie was half sitting, and Deanna used the back of the couch to hold the top of her body up as she continued to rub against Jamie. Jamie's mouth was close enough to kiss; her chest heaved against Deanna's, and Deanna dropped her gaze to watch as Jamie wet her dry lips with her tongue. Deanna wanted to press her mouth against Jamie's, wanted to crawl inside and devour her from the inside out, but more than that she wanted to watch Jamie as Deanna made her fall apart.

As she increased her pace, Jamie's hips rose up to meet Deanna's thigh. Deanna spared a moment to wonder if the rough material of Jamie's jeans would be too harsh on such a delicate part of her body. But the way Jamie had begun to pant, with her head thrown back and baring the long line of her throat, had Deanna thinking that even if it did hurt, it certainly wasn't taking anything away from the experience for Jamie.

Deanna's nightgown had ridden up, and as she pushed against Jamie she wanted more contact. Grabbing Jamie's hand, she pressed it against the bared skin of the back of her thigh. Jamie understood immediately and brought her other hand up as well, cupping the back of Deanna's ass as Jamie's movements under Deanna became more frantic.

Knowing she was close, Deanna grabbed a fistful of Jamie's hair, twisted her fingers in the thick strands and forced Jamie's head up so she could watch.

Jamie's teeth dug into her bottom lip. The expression on her face was torn between pain and pleasure, and, when Deanna leaned in closer and breathed "Now," against her mouth, Jamie came with a shuddering jerk.

Deanna rose and slid out of the bed before Jamie had begun to recover her breath. Jamie's breasts still strained against the fabric of her T-shirt as her lungs worked to suck in more air. Jamie's eyes had fallen shut, and when Deanna crawled back into the bed Jamie didn't bother to open them.

Deanna set her purple vibrator down on the bed beside her and reached for the hem of Jamie's shirt. Jamie lifted a hand, whether in protest or something else Deanna wasn't sure, because as Deanna worked the shirt up Jamie's torso, Jamie let her hand fall back to the bed.

Pleased to see that Jamie wore a bra with a front clasp, Deanna undid the garment and pushed it aside. Jamie's T-shirt was bunched up under her arms, and Deanna considered pulling it off but couldn't deny that she appreciated the way it made Jamie look utterly debauched. The flush from her orgasm was still hot, and it had made its way down her chest so that Deanna could nearly feel the heat radiating against her.

"What are you doing?" Jamie managed when Deanna moved down the bed to work at the top button on Jamie's jeans. "Let me—" she gestured toward Deanna, but Deanna brushed her hand away, then kissed the taut skin of Jamie's belly, just above the elastic band of her underwear.

"No, I want to take you apart," Deanna said with a shake of her head. "I want to make you come until you can't move. I want to leave you wrecked and still wanting more." Her lips curled into a smile against Jamie's skin. "Is that okay?" She looked up the lean, muscular line of Jamie's body and waited until she'd received Jamie's nod of assent.

"Good." Deanna dropped another kiss onto Jamie's abdomen; her tongue flicked out wetly against the skin in praise, and she purred low in her throat when Jamie twitched under her. She slid down the zipper of Jamie's jeans and eased them over her hips; she let her tongue trace the progress of bared flesh until she had them all the way off.

Jamie's legs had settled back together and, though Jamie began to open them, Deanna straddled Jamie's knees, keeping them pressed close. She brushed her lips against Jamie's, sliding deeper when Jamie parted hers in response.

The kiss was long and wet, a slow pull of heat that echoed the warmth in Deanna's center, and when she finally pulled back they were both breathless.

Deanna rested her forehead against Jamie's as she brought her hands up to cup Jamie's breasts, then dragged her thumbs over Jamie's nipples to feel Jamie writhe underneath her. Deanna now knew that Jamie liked her sex with an edge of teeth and nails, and it gave Deanna a perverse sort of pleasure to pet Jamie gently until she was nearly frantic with the need for more.

"Don't be a tease," Jamie warned, as though she had read Deanna's mind, her voice low and rough.

"Who, me?" Deanna was all innocence as she rubbed her lips against the shell of Jamie's ear, sucking the soft lobe and giving it a quick nip that had Jamie's breath catching. Her legs still squeezed tight around Jamie, Deanna slid her hand down Jamie's front and over the top of her underwear, one finger sliding between the V of Jamie's thighs.

Jamie's underwear was damp, and Deanna pressed her finger against the center of all that heat. Jamie's hips jerked at the touch as her legs tried to part, but Deanna held her fast. Leaning back so that she could again watch Jamie's face, Deanna began to move that single finger, rubbing against Jamie's clit through the fabric of her underwear.

Unlike earlier, when Jamie's jeans were between her and the blunt pressure of Deanna's thigh, Deanna's sensitive fingertip could feel Jamie swollen and wet through the material. She could feel every tiny shudder that ran through the other woman, smell the heavy scent of her desire, and when Deanna used her other hand to circle Jamie's throat, she could feel Jamie's pulse, rabbit-quick, under her fingers.

Jamie swore, hips bucking as she tried to increase the pressure at her clit. Deanna moved her hand faster, pressing closer until she could feel Jamie's thighs quake as she arched up and came with a strangled moan.

Deanna slid free and brought both hands up to cup Jamie's face. Jamie's skin was hot and damp under Deanna's touch, and her mouth was completely pliant. Deanna kissed her slowly, thoroughly and meticulously while Jamie shuddered under her with aftershocks.

When Deanna finally pulled back, Jamie reached for her again. This time Deanna let her stroke a hand languidly down Deanna's side, but when Jamie tried to draw her close Deanna wouldn't let her.

"I'm not done yet," she murmured, pulling Jamie's shirt and bra all the way off before leaning back to pull off her own nightgown. Jamie took advantage of her momentary distraction to dart forward and latch her mouth around Deanna's bared nipple. Deanna bit back a moan at the pull, tossed her nightgown to the floor and swayed forward into Jamie.

Jamie's hands came up and she tried to reverse their positions. Deanna wriggled free. "Not done yet," she reminded Jamie.

"Dee," Jamie pleaded, but Deanna shook her head, gesturing for Jamie to lie back as Deanna reached for the vibrator. Ripping open the package of a condom she'd brought from the bathroom, Deanna slid it over the toy before pressing it between Jamie's splayed legs.

At the first touch of the vibrating toy Jamie gave a choked moan and threw an arm over her eyes. Her entire body tensed as Deanna used two fingers to part Jamie's slick folds and moved the tip of the toy against Jamie's sensitive and swollen clit. Jamie jerked under Deanna; her body nearly twisted itself into knots as she tried to both push into and get away from the vibrations.

It took only a handful of seconds while Deanna gently circled Jamie's clit with the vibrator before she gave a hoarse cry and went limp. Deanna bent down and slid the flat of her tongue over Jamie, making a soft noise of satisfaction at the taste of her. Jamie's hand came down to rest against Deanna's hair, and when Deanna licked her again Jamie's fingers tightened, trying to pull Deanna back as a whimper of pleasure spilled from Jamie's mouth.

Deanna laughed against Jamie's wet heat, throbbing hot and heavy between her own legs as that light breath of air made Jamie's thighs shake around Deanna. Refusing to give Jamie the reprieve she was asking for, Deanna moved the vibrator lower and began to slowly work the head of it into Jamie. She'd turned it off after Jamie's first orgasm—well, Jamie's first orgasm with the vibrator, Deanna thought smugly—so when Jamie's spine bowed back from the sensation of something thick and unyielding pushing its way inside of her, Deanna nearly came just from watching Jamie. Her head was thrown back, her arm was still over her eyes and her chest heaved as Deanna continued to press in the vibrator until it was fully seated.

"Please," Jamie's hips rolled, trying to increase the pressure, to work the toy over that spot inside her. "Deanna. Please."

Deanna shifted, hiking one of Jamie's legs up against her shoulder and deepening the angle so that Jamie cried out under her, falling back against the bed with her hands clawing at the sheets. Deanna turned on the toy, and Jamie convulsed, her eyes flying open with a sharp cry as she arched up from the bed.

Deanna kept her eyes on Jamie's face as she fucked her with the buzzing toy, rubbing over and over her G-spot. Jamie reached out, and Deanna grasped her hand, nails digging into her skin as Jamie bit hard enough into her own lip that Deanna could see a dark bead of blood spill. Deanna shortened the strokes of the vibrator, keeping it close and tight against Jamie's G-spot, and, with something that was close to a scream, Jamie came.

Turning the toy off, Deanna slid it out of Jamie's body, then kissed softly and slowly against Jamie's belly before she worked her way up Jamie's limp form to press her mouth against Jamie's.

She'd expected to taste pennies, sweet and metallic from Jamie's blood, but to Deanna's surprise Jamie tasted only of the wine they'd had. Deanna was glad she'd only imagined the blood. That was a weird thing to imagine during sex, and she was pleased that Jamie hadn't actually hurt herself.

Tucked against Jamie's side, Deanna slid her hand between her own legs and pressed against her clit, where her fingers rubbed quickly and efficiently as she sought some relief from her own arousal. Beside her, Jamie twitched and then made a noise that Deanna could have sworn was a growl.

Before Deanna knew what was happening, Jamie had risen over her, shoving between her legs and pushing two fingers straight into her core. Deanna yelped, shock and pleasure blurring her vision as Jamie pumped into her relentlessly. When her vision started to clear, Deanna could see Jamie over her, her teeth bared in a fierce grin as Deanna writhed helplessly against her, and her eyes—her burning bourbon eyes—were now a pale, winter-sky gray.

Deanna's breath caught in her throat; confusion warred with the sensations of her body as Jamie added a third finger and Deanna's eyes rolled back into her head. Jamie bent over and sucked Deanna's clit into her mouth; her teeth grazed over the sensitive flesh, and, with a violent shudder, Deanna came in a hot flood.

Chapter Eight |

"I DON'T KNOW WHY YOU can't get your big butch girlfriend to help you hang another painting," Nathan complained as they headed into Deanna's building. "Isn't that the whole point of big butch girlfriends?"

"It's certainly a perk," Deanna agreed. She stopped in the lobby to check her mailbox. She knew she had the key *somewhere* in her purse. "But she's spending the weekend working on her seminar presentation, and I know it's been stressing her out lately, so I'm not going to bother her with this. Plus," she added, happy to have found the key. "We haven't been dating that long. We haven't used the 'G' word yet."

"I'd like to be able to use the 'G' word. Or the 'B' word," Nathan said morosely, leaning against the wall with the new canvas as he waited for Deanna to pull out her mail.

"I told you to try Tinder." Deanna stuffed the few envelopes under her arm and picked up the growler of beer she was using to bribe Nathan.

"That's hardly romantic." Nathan followed her up the stairs, and Deanna was glad he was bitching about his love life instead of the seven flights. "I mean, what's the point in being open and interested in the entire alphabet of sexuality if you still have to use the Internet to date?

God, I sound like an old man," he realized as they made their way down the hallway to Deanna's apartment. "I'm that old, crotchety man. 'In my day, we had to ask people out over the phone!'" he mimicked. "'These kids and their texts and their sexts! It's immoral!'"

"Uh huh," Deanna agreed absently, once she'd unlocked the door and let them in. After putting the beer down on the table, she flipped through the mail. Nathan continued to amuse himself and Arthur with what was now a monologue about the various pros and cons of the Internet. Bank statement, flyer for the pizza place, reminder about the city's upcoming changes to the curbside recycling program, and a large, hand-addressed envelope with no return address.

Curiosity piqued, Deanna trailed after Nathan with the beer and the envelope. Nathan relieved her of the growler and headed into the kitchen for glasses. Deanna tore open the seal, dumping the contents onto the coffee table.

A folded piece of paper fluttered out, accompanied by what looked like two photographs that had fallen onto the table face down. *Curiouser and curiouser*, Deanna mused, turning over the first photo and letting out a sudden, violent expletive when she saw her own image.

It was a candid shot, taken of Deanna and Arthur outside their building. She was wearing her bright red raincoat and carrying a bag of Arthur's dog food. She had no idea when it had been taken. She had no idea someone had taken her picture.

Nathan hastened out of the kitchen and, before Deanna could pick it up, grabbed the second picture. He turned it over, and his face went pale.

Deanna scowled and reached for it, but Nathan stepped back, shaking his head. "No, you don't want to see this one." Deanna ignored him and grabbed for it again.

"No." Nathan's good nature had vanished, and he was uncharacteristically fierce. "Not going to happen."

"Nathan, give me the fucking picture."

"Deanna—"

They were interrupted by a knock. Nathan's eyes went wide and he gestured for Deanna to stay still as he turned for the door.

Deanna's lips thinned into a hard line, and she followed right behind Nathan. She tried to shove past him, but Nathan pushed her back hard enough that Deanna made an outraged noise of pain and was sure she'd have a bruise.

"Who's there?" Nathan asked, not bothering to look through the peephole, but watching Deanna with unreadable eyes.

"It's Jamie. Can I come in?" Jamie's tone was strangely cautious, and Deanna tried again to grab the photo from Nathan. Deanna wasn't going to let Jamie see something Nathan was afraid to show her.

Nathan whipped the picture behind his back before unlocking the door and opening it a careful inch until he could see that it was Jamie.

Jamie eased through, clicking the lock behind her, which Deanna thought was odd. Jamie wasn't dressed to go out—she was barefoot, wearing only a pair of worn jeans that hung low on her hips and a green T-shirt frayed around the hem. Her hair wasn't styled, and if it hadn't been impossible Deanna might have thought that Jamie had come rushing in response to Deanna's reaction to the photo of her and Arthur. But obviously it was just a weird coincidence because, though Jamie was only one floor above her, Deanna was fairly certain Jamie couldn't hear every word spoken in her apartment.

"I just wanted to borrow some, um…" Jamie looked blankly around the apartment. "Dish soap."

"Now's not really the best—" Deanna began.

"Deanna just got this in the mail," Nathan handed Jamie the picture. Jamie was unnaturally still as she stared at the photo. With an angry huff, Deanna yanked it out of Jamie's hands.

It took a second to make sense of what she was looking at; the image in front of her was a mess of colors and shapes before it snapped into focus and bile rose thick in her throat.

It was a woman—it had been a woman—her body naked and pale against a cement floor. The reason it had taken Deanna a moment to understand what she was looking at was that the body—*her* body; whoever it was deserved to be thought of as more than *it*, a part of Deanna thought fiercely—had been torn at with such ferocity that Deanna thought there might actually be parts missing. Blood pooled dark under her; streaks of it were shockingly red against the poor woman's pale skin. What could do something like that to a person? The only comparison her stunned mind could draw was to a photo of a deer carcass she'd seen once, after a pack of wolves had been at it.

The worst part, though, if anything about the picture could be worse than any other part, was that where the woman's face should have turned toward the camera, someone had clumsily photoshopped Deanna's face instead.

Deanna was numb; white flickered at the edges of her vision as she tried to understand what was happening.

"There was a letter, too," Nathan crossed the room and picked up the folded piece of paper. He licked his lips, shot Deanna an uneasy glance and, after giving it a quick scan, passed it over.

Deanna took the paper without a word, standing stiffly as Jamie moved behind her to read over her shoulder.

Deanna. What a pretty name for a pretty girl. Too bad you won't be pretty for long. You are a stupid bitch cunt like the rest of them, but I thought maybe you'd listen to me. I've told you to stop. I was nice. I asked politely but you kept shutting me down, you kept trying to shut me up. I won't be censored, D. The truth doesn't hide. Do you see the truth in front of you now? DO YOU FUCKING GET IT? Wolf's Run isn't real, it's a farce, an INSULT, and if you keep allowing these human SHEEP to pretend they are something they ARE NOT I will show you what a REAL WOLF can do—just like I've showed the other stupid bitch cunts who won't open their EYES and BELIEVE.

See you soon – crywolf

Another picture, this time taped to the bottom of the page: a cut-out of a pair of someone's eyes. Whoever it was must have been wearing contacts, because his eyes were a strange, almost orange-gold that Deanna knew couldn't be natural.

Behind her, Jamie inhaled sharply and stumbled back, nearly tripping over Nathan's shoes.

"It's not that bad," Deanna said tonelessly. "He's said worse. If it weren't for the pictures, it would just be more of the same."

"We have to call the police." Nathan was already looking up the non-emergency police number. "He's stalking you. This isn't some cyberbullying trolling crap anymore, this is real."

"So he keeps insisting." Deanna was oddly calm. The note wasn't as bad as some of his tweets had been. But the pictures…

Nathan began to speak to whoever had picked up on the other end and turned away to pace in front of Deanna's windows. Deanna tuned out his words, not wanting to hear what he was telling the police, and focused on Jamie, who still hadn't said a word.

"Are you okay?" Deanna reached out and was surprised when Jamie flinched away. "It's not—I mean, it's fucked up, and creepy, but." Deanna shrugged, trying to shake it off. "I'm okay."

Jamie stared at her before she shook her head. "It's not. This is serious, Deanna. He knows where you *live*."

"Yes, and all he did was send me a nasty letter and take a couple of pictures. I'm not taking this lightly," she added when Jamie opened her mouth again. "We'll report it. But this guy is a coward hiding behind a computer screen. It's not hard to find pictures like… like that," she gestured at the second picture she'd placed face down on the side table.

"I don't think—" Jamie began, but Nathan had ended his call and strode toward them. He gathered up the envelope and plucked the letter from Deanna's fingers.

"Come on, they want us to go down to the station."

Glad she'd kept her shoes on, Deanna picked up her purse and thought, distantly, that she was never going to get her new painting hung.

Chapter Nine |

"You should quit."

Deanna glanced up from where she was washing the dinner dishes in Jamie's sink. "I'm almost done. I know you think they can wait, but I can't stand leaving dirty dishes overnight. Plus, you cooked for me, so it's really the least I can do."

"No, I don't mean—" Jamie took a breath. She was sitting at her kitchen table, her foot tapping a restless beat against the tile. Arthur was alert on his belly beside her. "You should quit your job," she clarified, not quite looking Deanna in the eye.

Deanna arched an incredulous eyebrow over her glasses. She'd traded her contacts for them when they'd returned from the station. "You sound like the detective who told me to just 'stop using the Internet for a while.' And trust me, you sound as ridiculous as he did." Although the police had been polite enough, there apparently hadn't been anything they could do. Without an ID for crywolf she would have a tough time seeking a restraining order, and that was apparently the only recourse against someone who was "only" accused of stalking. They'd made copies of the letter and the pictures, and had created a file. But otherwise they had been entirely unhelpful, not to mention time-consuming.

"This is serious, Dee."

"I *know* it's serious, Jamie." Deanna reminded herself to be patient. Jamie was concerned, and it was clear now that concern when it came to crywolf was well founded. "Quitting my job isn't the answer, though."

"It's what he wants. If you quit, maybe he'll stop."

"He doesn't want me to quit; he wants the whole game to quit. And that's not going to happen." *Wolf's Run* was gaining popularity, and there was talk on the admin boards that it might hit number one on the top ten list for role-playing games in Vancouver. Right now they were hovering at number five.

"I'm worried."

"I'm worried too. But that doesn't mean I'm going to let an idiot with an Internet connection and Photoshop dictate my actions." Deanna tugged off her rubber gloves as she turned to face Jamie.

"It's more dangerous than that." Jamie pushed her chair back with uncharacteristic force, and the chair legs squeaked against the tile.

"I'm a woman with an active online presence. Do you think I haven't received death threats before? Worse?" Deanna shrugged.

"Not like this you haven't." Jamie's words rang with certainty.

"Because he used snail mail instead of email? You know what—don't answer. It doesn't matter. I'm not quitting my job." Deanna dropped the pink rubber gloves beside the sink. She'd brought them after the first time Jamie had cooked for her, when she'd discovered that Jamie seemed to have no regard for the delicate skin of her hands, plunging them into near scalding water without so much as a blink. That was how she took care of Jamie. That was how you took care of someone you were in a relationship with—not by telling them to quit doing what they wanted to do, but by helping them do it well.

Deanna crossed the kitchen and knelt in front of Jamie. "Let this drop, okay?" She ran her hands over Jamie's thighs, and was surprised at the tension she could feel through the fabric of Jamie's jeans.

"I want you to at least consider it. Deanna, you don't realize what—"

"Stop it, Jamie."

On the floor, Arthur gave a nervous whine, his gaze jumping between the two of them.

"I need you to listen to me." Jamie was rigid, her hand flexing into a fist on the table as though she didn't know what to do with it.

"And I need you to stop. This is kind of out of line."

"Out of line?" It was Jamie's turn to sound incredulous. "I'm trying to keep you safe."

"I don't need you to protect me."

"You do, Dee. This time you really do. You just have to trust me on this, please."

"I trust you, Jamie. But I need you to trust me as well, okay? And that means letting me make my own decisions—even if you don't agree with them." Deanna stood. "I appreciate you offering to let us stay here tonight, but Arthur and I are going to go back downstairs."

"Deanna."

Deanna shook her head, already moving toward the door. The pleading note in Jamie's voice almost made Deanna change her mind, but she was too tired to want to spend the night arguing with Jamie.

"Not tonight, Jamie." Deanna picked up her purse from the couch. Arthur was close on her heels as she toed on her shoes.

Jamie sat at the table, not looking at Deanna, and, with a sigh, Deanna left.

Chapter Ten |

I KNOW YOU'RE SITTING IN your bed moping but that's enough of that.

Deanna scowled at the text Nathan had sent her before tossing her phone onto the pillow next to her. Nathan didn't know she was in bed. She could have turned it back into the couch. Or be sitting at her desk. Maybe she wasn't even home. She needed to get groceries—it was actually ridiculous how many groceries a person needed to buy—so for all Nathan knew she could be out shopping.

Stop ignoring me.

Deanna.

Deaaaaaaaaaaaaaaannnnnaaaaaaaa.

I'm outside and I can see the light in your window. If you don't put on pants and come down I'm going to ring your buzzer until the sound of it drives you insane and then you'll have an actual reason to mope.

Deanna made an inarticulate noise of irritation and debated turning her phone off. But Nathan had been good not to check up on her until now. She'd texted him last night when she'd left Jamie's to bemoan the fact that they'd had their first fight. Since she'd ignored her phone all day, she supposed she owed it to him to get up.

Fine. She rolled out of bed.

Good. And bring Arthur. You two are coming over for Pasta à la Nathan and a *Girls* marathon.

Of course he'd know the exact combination that would be enticing enough to convince her to go with him.

Give me fifteen minutes to shower.

I'll be waiting, was his prompt reply.

It took Deanna only a couple of minutes to pull her wet hair up into a bun and throw on a pair of leggings and the large, zip-up hoodie that Jamie had left behind the last time she'd stayed over.

Snapping on Arthur's leash, she grabbed her bag and turned off the overhead light. At the last minute, she flicked on the small lamp she kept at her desk. She didn't relish the idea of coming home to a dark apartment, even though crywolf had been quiet since she'd received his hate mail.

"Here." The second she stepped outside, Nathan thrust a shopping bag at her. "You can help me carry dinner."

Deanna made a face but took the bag with her free hand as they headed down the street. Nathan's place wasn't close, but with a dog they couldn't hop into one of the city's car shares, so it was easiest to walk. Between crywolf's letter and Deanna spending today brooding about Jamie, she figured it was probably for the best, anyway.

Nathan didn't ask Deanna how she was doing; instead he kept up a stream of chatter about his day at work and the latest university library gossip. By the time they got to his place, a trendy studio loft in an industrial quarter of the city that was gradually filling with art galleries and craft breweries, Deanna felt better than she had in days.

As comfortable in his place as he was in hers, she helped him put away the groceries. Arthur, equally comfortable, sprawled in the middle of the floor so that as Nathan prepared their meal he had to engage in a careful dance of don't-trip-over-the-dog.

Holding the glass of Chianti Nathan had poured for her, Deanna settled in with her back against the counter to watch Nathan wash vegetables, juggle cookware and chop.

"It's a crime against nature that someone hasn't snapped you up yet," she opined.

"Or several someones," Nathan agreed, blue eyes twinkling through his glasses. "I guess the universe is holding out for someone special."

"Probably." Deanna laughed. The last person Nathan had dated was a professional contortionist. While Deanna was obviously biased, she thought Nathan would either wind up with an actual prince or remain single, and die with a string of ex-lovers weeping hysterically at his funeral. He was just that sort of person—settling for less would never occur to him.

"Speaking of someone special…" Nathan shot her a meaningful glance as he set onions and garlic hissing and spitting in a skillet.

Deanna sighed, knowing her reprieve had been too good to last. "She keeps texting. And calling. But I don't want to talk about it anymore, so…" She shrugged gracelessly.

Nathan added the rest of the ingredients to the skillet before picking up his own glass of wine and turning to face Deanna. "You should let her know you're okay, at least."

"I know." Deanna looked away guiltily. When she got home, she'd send Jamie a text and see if the other woman wanted to go for coffee in the morning. If Jamie agreed to respect Deanna's decision to continue working for *Wolf's Run*, then everything could go back to normal. Deanna really, really missed normal with Jamie. Which, since it had been barely twenty-four hours since their sort-of-fight, meant Deanna was falling. Hard. She took a big gulp of the wine and set the table.

"You really didn't have to walk me home," Deanna told Nathan for the tenth time at the door to her building. "It's not like I haven't made my way back from your place before."

"Yeah, well, there hasn't been a psycho stalking you before."

"That we know of." Deanna winked, deciding that if she did actually have a stalker she might as well be able to joke about it. Luckily, Nathan was her kind of person; as she fished in her bag for her keys, he struck an obnoxious pose on the steps.

"I want to make sure he gets my good side," he informed her, though Deanna didn't miss the shrewd way his blue eyes scanned the other side of the street.

"Thank you for dinner." She drew him close, and he gave her a giant squeeze, dropping a kiss on her forehead.

"Take care of my favorite person and my favorite dog," he told her as she opened the door and let Arthur in.

"Promise," Deanna called over her shoulder, rolling her eyes to disguise how touched she was that he'd gone all the way to her place and back just to make sure she got home safe, and that now he even waited until the door had closed and locked itself behind her.

Distractedly composing the text she planned to send to Jamie, Deanna didn't let Arthur off his leash until she pulled open the door to their floor and he practically yanked it out of her hands. Startled, she looked up to see what was causing him to pull so intently only to see Jamie scrambling to her feet from where she'd been sitting in the hall outside Deanna's door.

So much for the text. Not entirely sure how she felt, she kept a tight hold on Arthur's leash as they made their way down the hall toward Jamie.

The habitually well-groomed woman looked like shit. Her eyes were bloodshot, her flannel button-up was wrinkled, and the look on her face was one of such intense relief that Deanna wondered if she hadn't missed a natural disaster or terrorist attack.

"I didn't know where you were," Jamie said, her voice cracking. "You didn't answer your phone, and you weren't in your apartment, and I didn't know..." She was tight with tension, hands shaking, and it looked as though it was all she could do not to reach out for Deanna.

"I was at Nathan's," Deanna said carefully. "My phone was in my bag."

"Okay." Jamie took a step back, shoved her hands into the pockets of her jeans and hunched her shoulders. "Okay."

"Are you?" Deanna asked. "Okay?" Her own fingers wrapped tightly around the strap of her bag and Arthur's leash. She wanted to pull Jamie into a hug and tell her that they were all right, that everything was all right, but wasn't sure if either of those things were actually true.

"No," Jamie admitted, guilelessly. "I'm not. I need to talk to you. Can I come in?"

Deanna glanced at her door. She didn't need a repeat of the other night, and the last thing she wanted to do was to ask Jamie to leave her apartment.

"Please. It's serious." Jamie pressed her arms closer to her body as if she was trying to make herself seem smaller. "I need to tell you something."

Deanna blew out a long breath. It wasn't the discussion over coffee that she'd imagined, but it didn't seem as though Jamie would be able to wait. "Okay."

She'd thought agreeing would ease some of Jamie's tension, but now Jamie seemed strung even tighter. With an apprehensive knot forming in her own stomach, Deanna unlocked the door and let Arthur and Jamie in.

After unclipping Arthur's leash and pulling off the hoodie—and hoping Jamie wouldn't recognize it as hers—Deanna tossed her purse onto the side table and headed into the main room, which, she remembered with a mental groan, was her bedroom since she hadn't folded up the sofa bed. She flicked on the light and hoped Jamie would ignore the disarray. Considering that Jamie herself seemed to be a mess, the odds were good.

"What's going on?" she asked, turning to face Jamie and unable to hide the concern in her voice.

Their fight last night—and really, it had been more of a disagreement than an actual fight—hadn't been pleasant, but Deanna didn't think it had been bad enough to cause this level of anxiety in Jamie. Jamie's arms were still hugged tight at her sides, and she held her body as though it was something brittle waiting for a blow.

"You, uh, should probably sit down," Jamie said, a ghost of a wry grin flickering over her face.

"You're not pregnant, are you?" Deanna joked halfheartedly—though even as she said it, a spark of alarm shot through her. Jamie couldn't be, could she?

"No." This time Jamie almost laughed. "No, it's not that. God. I don't exactly know how to say this." She ran her fingers through her hair, turning to stare at her own reflection in the window. "I haven't had to do this. I haven't had to tell anyone. It's not something you really think you'll ever have to do, you know?"

"Um, sure?" It was cancer, wasn't it? Jamie was dying from some sort of wasting illness, and she and Deanna had just fought, and now Deanna was going to feel like a monster for being angry at her girlfriend for just wanting to keep her safe when Jamie was the one who was dying. If so, Deanna definitely wanted to be sitting down, so, with trepidation weighing heavy in the pit of her stomach, she eased herself onto the edge of the mattress.

"Fuck." Jamie drew Deanna's curtains and turned back. From the pale, hollow look on her face, Deanna expected her to be sick any minute.

"Hey, listen, it's gonna be okay. Whatever it is, we can—" Deanna started.

"No." Jamie shook her head, cutting her off. "Let me talk, all right? It's just going to sound crazy. And you're going to think it's a joke or that I'm making fun of you, but I swear it's nothing like that, okay? It's just—it's important that you know. And it's important that no one else does."

Deanna gave a slow nod, clasped her hands in her lap and waited.

"I'm a werewolf."

Deanna stared at her. "What?"

"I'm a werewolf," Jamie repeated.

Deanna blew out a slow breath. "First you think the situation with crywolf is so serious that I need to *quit my job* over it, and now you're making jokes?" She was at a loss to understand what was going on in Jamie's head, but was doing her best to "find her calm," as Nathan put it.

"Deanna, I'm not joking."

"Yeah, and I'm a vampire. And Arthur's actually a shapeshifter. Oh, and Heather across the hall is a mummy. Ha, ha, ha." Deanna arched an eyebrow. "What is going on with you?"

"Listen to me. I turn into a wolf. An actual wolf. With fur, and fangs, and—"

"Let me guess, they're all the better to eat me with?" Deanna gave a weak laugh. "Can we stop? Please?"

Instead of saying anything, Jamie began to unbutton her shirt. Unable to sit still any longer, Deanna leapt off the bed. "What are you doing? Are you on something?" Nathan had done—still did—some strange drugs, so Deanna wasn't unfamiliar with the concept of a bad trip. "Sit down and I'll get you a glass of water, and then maybe you can sleep." *And sleep it off.*

Jamie shook her head. "I'm going to show you."

"You're going to show me that you're a werewolf." Maybe if she said it enough, Jamie would realize how absurd she sounded.

Jamie said nothing, refusing to meet Deanna's gaze as she pulled off her shirt and dropped it on the floor at her feet. She hadn't worn a bra, and as her hands moved to the waistband of her jeans, Deanna jerked her eyes away. She'd watched Jamie get undressed dozens of times, but never felt as intrusive as she did right now. No matter what it might look like to an outside observer, there was nothing sexual about the way Jamie pushed her jeans down her hips, as if she'd rather be doing anything but this.

"I'm serious. This is actually insane. Please stop," Deanna pleaded. "Whatever's going on, we'll talk about it. Just stop."

Jamie placed her jeans on top of her shirt, stepped out of her underwear and tugged off her socks until she stood completely naked in front of Deanna. "I'm sorry," she said.

"It's okay. Let me get you a robe, all right? You can sit down and we'll—"

Jamie wasn't listening. She closed her eyes and let her hands fall to her sides. For a moment nothing happened, and Deanna rubbed wearily at her mouth. Maybe she needed to call Nathan and get him back here.

Between one second and the next, Jamie's entire body just—crumpled in on itself.

A strangled scream choked itself off in Deanna's throat as she jerked back in horror. Her calves hit the edge of the bed, spilling her back onto the mattress with enough force that the breath left her body in a rush.

Deanna pushed herself up on her elbows as she gasped for air. Her eyes were wide and glassy. Fur crawled over the misshapen thing that had once been a perfectly ordinary human body. Jamie—because no matter what Deanna's eyes were telling her, it had to still be Jamie—gave a shuddering twitch, and suddenly her limbs became limbs again. Only they weren't human arms and legs, they were very clearly canine. *Or, lupine*, a small, hysterical voice inside Deanna corrected.

Arthur gave a welcoming yip and bounded past Deanna to sniff delightedly at the, well, *wolf* that was standing on four clawed feet on Deanna's apartment floor. Wolf-Jamie gave a quick wag of her tail and a lick to Arthur's head before she carefully sat down and stared at Deanna.

Chapter Eleven |

"WELL, THAT... HAPPENED," DEANNA MANAGED faintly. Her ears rang in the echoing silence of the room. Jamie said nothing. Obviously. Because she was a wolf. And wolves didn't speak. Or they couldn't speak English, anyway. Unless werewolves had English-compatible voice boxes? Deanna could feel that small thread of hysteria becoming bigger and she clamped her mouth shut on the trilling laugh that bubbled in her throat.

As a wolf—a werewolf—Jamie was over twice the size of Arthur. Maybe three times bigger if Deanna counted not just height, but girth as well. Jamie's eyes were no longer the heady bourbon-brown Deanna was used to, but a clear, icy gray that looked oddly familiar. She was white around her muzzle, brownish-tan ran up the bridge of her nose, darker gray masked her eyes and brindled fur continued down her sides and, presumably, her back.

Deanna sat up, her brain buzzing with blank static. "Does this mean what I think it means?" she asked absently. "Did the *Twilight* books get something right?"

Jamie's jaw parted to reveal a set of wicked white fangs before her tongue lolled out, and Deanna thought that meant she might be laughing.

"Holy shit. Holy fucking shit." Deanna reached out a hand before she could think better of it, her fingers trembling. With a cautious movement, as if trying not to scare Deanna, Jamie dropped her head so that Deanna could touch her.

Jamie's fur was coarser than Arthur's, thick and heavy under the palm of Deanna's hand. As she stroked it, she felt for all the world as if she were petting a giant dog.

"Okay. Um. Well." Deanna swallowed and tried to get a handle on what had just happened. "So you're a werewolf. That's a thing. A thing that people can be." She pulled her hand away, staring at her own palm as if she'd never seen it. "Okay. Wow."

Jamie shifted, and Deanna figured it was as close to a shrug as she could manage now that she had four legs. Deanna flattened her hand against the bed, not entirely sure what to do now. What did you say to your girlfriend, who had literally turned into a bitch in front of your eyes? Especially when it seemed she couldn't say anything back?

Jamie made a low noise in her throat, not quite a whine, but didn't move from where she sat on Deanna's floor.

"Um. I think it would be good if you went back to being human for now. If you can?"

Jamie nodded—weird, seeing a giant wolf nod—and backed up. Deanna took a deep breath and steeled herself, half wanting to look away but horribly fascinated, as Jamie seemed to expand and then shrink and the coat of fur vanished. As suddenly as she'd shifted the first time, Jamie was crouched naked and human on the hardwood.

"Hi," Deanna said, her eyes so round she could feel them bulging and thought they might fall right out of their sockets.

"Hey," Jamie replied softly, staying small and crouched as though unsure how Deanna would react, but ready to cringe away if need be.

"You could put your clothes back on," Deanna offered. "Or I could get you that robe. I don't… I mean… you… yeah," she trailed off, lamely. She thought she was in shock—though, unlike when she'd received the private message from crywolf or his letter in the mail, it wasn't panic-driven. Everything seemed a bit distant, as though she were experiencing the world through a clouded pane of thick glass.

Moving as cautiously as she had when clothed in her pelt, Jamie unfurled herself and tugged her clothes back on. Deanna didn't mean to keep watching her, meant to politely cast her gaze to the side, but she still couldn't reconcile the giant, furred *wolf* with the long-limbed, well-muscled, increasingly less-naked woman in front of her.

Fastening the last button on her shirt, Jamie straightened and remained standing at the window, her own gaze fixed on the bed sheets somewhere to the right of Deanna. Arthur was entirely unconcerned and flopped down on the floor between them, gave a giant yawn and then tucked his head between his front paws.

"Do you want me to go?" Jamie finally broke the silence. Her completely ordinary, human eyes flicked to Deanna's face.

"No." Deanna shook her head. "No. You should stay. Um… I feel like I should have a lot of questions." She gave a ghost of a smile. "But I kind of just want to sit for a bit, if that's okay."

"Sure." Jamie smoothed nervous fingers down the front of her shirt and moved to step around Arthur to the armchair in the corner.

Deanna still wasn't sure what was going on, and was at least partly convinced she was stuck in a really weird dream. But assuming that she wasn't, and assuming that her girlfriend was—and had been—a werewolf, Deanna didn't think starting another fight would help. If nothing that was happening made sense, then Deanna supposed it was up to her to make some kind of sense out of it. So she wasn't going to freak out about something so far beyond her control—and quite possibly out of Jamie's as well. She would try to digest this new information and keep everything else as normal as possible.

Jamie continued to hold herself as if ready for Deanna hit her or try to remove her from the apartment. Deanna was very sure she could do neither unless Jamie let her—suddenly Jamie's careless strength seemed all the more careless. If anything, Jamie seemed more fragile than Deanna felt, and the thought of Jamie thinking she needed to protect herself from Deanna, despite everything Deanna had just learned, made Deanna's heart ache. "You could sit with me?" she offered, finally.

Jamie froze while in the act of sitting in the armchair, her butt hanging awkwardly over the seat. Deanna might have laughed if the situation had been any different.

"I would like it if you'd sit with me," Deanna clarified. Everything still seemed oddly muffled, and she supposed it was her brain's way of protecting her from the complete bizarreness of what had just occurred. Jamie had clearly expected Deanna to take her being a werewolf as a deal-breaker for their relationship, and Deanna thought she probably would have a point there; but right now all Deanna wanted was her girlfriend, even if that girlfriend was a werewolf. Which was still an idea that didn't feel entirely real. Damn.

Jamie gave a slow nod and crawled into the bed, careful to leave plenty of room between herself and Deanna as she settled against the back of the couch. Deanna gave her a moment to get comfortable and then turned toward her, wriggling so that she was tucked against Jamie's side with her head resting just under Jamie's breasts and her arm wrapped around Jamie's middle.

Jamie froze at Deanna's first touch and stayed nearly rigid as tension thrummed through her body. After an agonizing minute, she warily brought her hand to rest on Deanna's shoulder and, when Deanna only nuzzled in closer, Jamie finally began to relax.

"Thank you for telling me," Deanna murmured against Jamie's ribs.

"Uh, you're welcome?" Jamie hedged. She had tensed again when Deanna spoke, but when Deanna said nothing further she calmed.

Jamie's thumb moved in slow circles over Deanna's skin and, with the steady thud of Jamie's heartbeat under her ear and her adrenaline rush fading fast, Deanna felt her eyes grow heavy. With a contented sigh, she closed them.

DEANNA WASN'T SURE HOW MUCH time had passed when she opened her eyes, but the room was dark. Arthur had blatantly disregarded all the rules and joined them on the bed; his furred back was curled against Deanna's.

With a sigh Deanna rolled over and shoved him toward the edge of the bed, then pushed until, with an undignified yelp, he tumbled off the side. "He knows better," she told Jamie, rolling back toward her and refusing to feel bad when Arthur gave a piteous whine at the indignity of having to stay on the floor while everyone else was on the bed. "Sorry I fell asleep." She flopped onto her back and stretched, feeling as though she'd been in the same position for hours. Which, considering the dryness in her mouth, she might have been.

"It's okay." Her expression unreadable, Jamie shifted away from Deanna. "How are you?"

Deanna considered. "All right. A little groggy. I hate waking up from naps."

"That's not—" Jamie broke off, her words sharp with frustration. "I mean how are you with *this*," she gestured to herself.

"With you?" Deanna asked, surprised. "Fine. Why wouldn't I be fine?"

"Because I just told you I was a *werewolf* and then actually *turned into a wolf* and you just… fell asleep."

"I guess I was more tired than I realized. Though," Deanna smiled, "you can't tell me that's not the best reaction you could have hoped for."

Jamie opened her mouth to counter this, but after a moment closed it.

Deanna shrugged. "I know I'm supposed to be accusing you of lying and feeling betrayed and possibly throwing things at your head, but it wouldn't change anything. You'd still be a werewolf, and I'd still be," *falling in love with you* was on the tip of her tongue, startling even herself; with a hasty swallow Deanna finished, "here. I'd still be here. So, how about we skip the whole yelling thing."

Jamie said nothing, and Deanna wondered if they were going to have a fight anyway. She couldn't deny that a part of her was freaking out—that in some corner of her mind she was panicking about the fact that when Jamie shifted, so had Deanna's entire world. But Jamie being a werewolf obviously didn't stop her from being incredibly human in so many other ways. She was strong, and smart and beautiful, and if the fact that she sometimes went furry didn't change any of those things, maybe it didn't have to change their relationship. Not if they didn't let it.

Jamie blew out a slow breath, though it didn't seem to relax her much. "All right. But… you'll talk to me, right? If you stop being so fine. You'll tell me?"

"I will," Deanna promised, and slid her fingers between Jamie's. "Thanks for sticking around."

"Of course." Jamie's fingers tightened around Deanna's as her expression went grim. "I don't want to leave you alone."

"Well," Deanna said dryly, pushing herself upright. "That got dark."

"You know *why* I had to tell you—right?"

"Because you finally felt like you could trust me, and didn't feel like keeping such a strange secret?" Deanna gave a weak smile, ignoring the weight of trepidation that settled in her chest.

Jamie didn't look as if she found Deanna amusing. "Because I think crywolf is one of us."

"Queer?" Deanna tried another joke, but it fell equally flat.

"A werewolf," Jamie clarified, mouth twisting unhappily.

Deanna sighed and tucked her knees up so she could rest her cheek against them, then turned to face Jamie. She was still being careful about her body language, and relatively careful about her actual language, because Jamie seemed wary enough to bolt if Deanna said the wrong thing. Not that she thought Jamie would leave the apartment—not after her last statement—but she might leave the bed.

"Okay. Like a werewolf you *know*, or just a werewolf, period." *Just a werewolf. Hah.*

"A werewolf. Period."

"Okay." Deanna sighed. "Now I have questions. But first," she said as she unfolded herself and crawled off the bed, then motioned for Jamie to stay where she was when Jamie began to follow her, "I want a glass of water. You?"

Jamie nodded, giving Deanna's hand another squeeze.

Deanna turned on the bedside lamp; the warm light cast the room in a cozy glow, and made the fact that they were about to have a serious discussion about *werewolves* seem even more ludicrous. After padding into the kitchen on bare feet, she pulled out two glasses, filled them with water, went back to the bed and passed one to Jamie.

Jamie gave a quick nod, not meeting Deanna's eyes. Despite Deanna's assurance that she could stay on the bed, Jamie had moved to sit on the edge of it and now radiated waves of tension. Deanna set her own glass down on the small table, pushed her way between Jamie's legs and forced the other woman to look up at her.

Moving slowly so that there could be no mistaking her intention, Deanna ran her fingers lightly through Jamie's mess of hair, then cupped the back of her head before she brought her lips down to kiss Jamie's mouth. Jamie was utterly still, but as Deanna tightened her fingers, Jamie's lips parted and she made a soft sound and moved her free hand to grasp the fabric of Deanna's tank top at the small of her back.

Deanna pulled away. "Still here," she murmured against Jamie's lips before she pulled back to retrieve her glass, settling cross-legged on the mattress. "Cheers," she said, tapping her glass to Jamie's.

"Cheers," Jamie echoed, her eyes still slightly unfocused in a way that made Deanna take a smug sip.

Deanna waited until Jamie had taken a drink. "What makes you think that crywolf is a werewolf?"

Jamie took another swallow. "His eyes—when he sent you those photographs, there was a picture glued to the bottom of the letter."

Deanna nodded. The police had been content to take a copy and hadn't seemed interested in keeping the original. She'd been tempted to throw it away, but Nathan had convinced her otherwise, and so it, along with the two other photographs, remained stuffed into Deanna's junk drawer. If she had to keep them, she wasn't going to keep them anywhere nice.

"That's one of the, ah… many things your game has wrong about werewolves," Jamie said diplomatically. "Our eyes are one of the first things to change. Plus, we're never, ever 'wolfmen.'" Jamie actually looked affronted by the suggestion.

"I suppose that's why he's so angry," Deanna reasoned. "If our portrayals are basically caricatures."

"Please," Jamie scoffed. "People are obsessed with the supernatural. If we got all bent out of shape over every inaccurate depiction of a werewolf, we'd never do anything else. It's no excuse for what he's doing."

"I didn't say that. He just seems slightly less crazy now that he's, you know, actually what he says he is."

"That shouldn't make you feel any safer. Someone with a weird obsession on the Internet might just stay weird and on the Internet— but this guy is taking it personally. I don't know why he's focused on *Wolf's Run*, and I have no clue why he's focused on you, but he is. And he's not crazy. You have to be careful, Deanna," Jamie stressed, moving forward to grip Deanna's knee. "You shouldn't go anywhere alone. And I think you've got to at least consider quitting *Wolf's Run*. I wouldn't have asked you to if I didn't believe it was this important."

Deanna didn't reply. The thought of quitting her job just because someone was harassing her made her hackles go up as though she were the wolf, not Jamie—but she couldn't deny that Jamie had a point.

If this guy was a werewolf, and could do what she'd seen Jamie do earlier—could wear the same fangs Jamie had sported earlier—Deanna had good reason to take his threats seriously. But let him control her life? No. She couldn't do it. She wouldn't.

"I won't be an idiot. I'm not going to take stupid risks," she began.

"Dee—"

"No," Deanna said firmly. "I won't quit my job. I understand now why you asked, but please don't ask me again."

Jamie looked ready to argue, but, to Deanna's relief, she bit her tongue.

"I'll be careful, though. And, I mean, we don't have proof that he's actually hurt anyone." Deanna's mind flicked to the picture he'd sent her and the woman who'd been torn to shreds. She'd never thought crywolf had been responsible for it, but now... well, now she wasn't so sure. "It could still blow over."

Jamie didn't look convinced. "He's chancing a lot, contacting you like he is. We have rules, and he's breaking them. He's going rogue. Gone rogue?" She gave a useless shrug. "I haven't heard of it happening in years." She looked as troubled as she had before she'd dropped the whole werewolf bomb. "I've asked my pack to reach out, to see if anyone knows who he is, or where."

"We're safe tonight though, right?" Deanna, hoping to ease the worried lines on her face, lifted Jamie's hand and dropped a quick kiss on her knuckles.

"I won't let anything happen to you," Jamie swore, with something fierce in her voice. Deanna had a flash of the large, deadly fangs that were as much a part of Jamie as her blunt, human teeth. She suppressed a shudder—not at what Jamie *could* do, but at what Jamie was obviously prepared to do. Deanna wasn't a complete moron. She had known from the pictures he'd sent her that crywolf was no longer a laughing matter, but he suddenly felt more real than anything else. Because not only did Jamie have fangs, crywolf probably did as well—and his could tear at Jamie as easily as hers could tear at him.

"Tell me more, though. How many werewolves are there? How big is your pack? Do you have an 'alpha'?" Deanna said the last word mockingly, finger quotes and all, and was astounded when Jamie actually blushed. "Oh, you're not serious," she groaned. "Alphas, really?"

"What? Pop culture had to get it right some time."

Chapter Twelve |

FOR ALL INTENTS AND PURPOSES, Jamie moved into Deanna's apartment. Deanna didn't have the room, not exactly, but they had managed to make it work for one week and were starting their second. If Nathan thought their sudden cohabitation was remarkable, he kept it to himself, winking cheekily at Deanna the next time he stopped by and was just in time to catch Jamie going to campus after having very clearly used Deanna's shower.

For the first few days Jamie had refused to leave Deanna's side, but having someone constantly underfoot—and the small size of Deanna's apartment meant Jamie would be in the way—had driven Deanna dangerously close to snapping. When Deanna had expressed this sentiment through gritted teeth and with an ominously raised spatula, Jamie had agreed to continue her schoolwork as usual. Deanna had reasoned with her that she was only a phone call away, and had sworn up and down that she wouldn't answer her door to anyone she didn't know or wasn't expecting. Besides, she doubted very much that a werewolf would stage an attack on her in the middle of the city and in broad daylight. Jamie had relented on the condition that she would be back at Deanna's apartment every evening at five on the dot.

Living with Jamie had been illuminating—and not just because Deanna learned several new and interesting places in her apartment they could have sex, but because it allowed Deanna to pepper Jamie with questions about her "furry little problem."

"My furry little *what*?"

"You know, like in *Harry Potter*. You did read *Harry Potter*, right?"

"Yeah. Once."

"Well, it's a literary classic so you should probably reread it. But Professor Lupin used to be friends with—you know what, never mind." The unimpressed expression on Jamie's face led Deanna to abandon her explanation and hasten to her question. "Wolfsbane: pretty or poison?"

"Pretty. Silver's the thing that really hurts." Jamie popped her earbud back in and returned to her research.

Deanna made a mental note to reorganize her jewelry box.

WEREWOLVES HAD ONLY THREE BIG rules, Deanna learned. One: protect your pack. Two: don't kill anyone. Three: don't get caught.

Jamie's pack was her family. Deanna had been only slightly disappointed to learn that it was impossible for a bite from a werewolf to turn a human into one, and that the ability was passed down from parent to child. Or grandparent to child—Jamie's mother was fully human, as well as her father. Both of her mother's siblings, Trevor of the "bored games" and the pack's current alpha, Michael, had the ability to shift, as had their mother, who was the previous alpha. Knowing that Jamie's father had married into a family of werewolves, aware and apparently unconcerned that his child could grow fur, made Deanna eager to meet him. Assuming, of course, that things continued to go so well with Jamie.

With one hand wrapped around Arthur's leash and the other tucked firmly into the crook of Jamie's arm, Deanna tried not to be too smug as they walked home from Granville Island's public market with

Jamie talking about the romantic comedy she was trying to convince Deanna to watch.

"I know you don't like Vince Vaughn—"

"He looks like how a pube in your mouth feels."

Jamie looked at Deanna askance and not a little horrified, but gamely continued. "*The Breakup* is incredibly underrated. I don't know if I've ever seen a movie with a more honest representation of—"

"I'll watch it if you watch *Jupiter Ascending*," Deanna offered smoothly, turning to Jamie with a winning smile.

Jamie's step faltered; a pained expression crossed her face as she weighed the pros and cons of sitting through more sci-fi. "I'll think about it," she said finally.

"Great." If someone had told Deanna a month ago that her quiet, mysterious, sexy upstairs neighbor had a weak spot for romcoms, of all things, Deanna wouldn't have believed it for a second. Somehow that seemed more out of character than the fact that Jamie could turn into a wolf.

Deciding it was time to change the subject before she had to hear more about Vince Vaughn, Deanna pointed with their joined hands to a man several meters away. He was talking on his cell phone, with one finger jabbing at the empty air in front of him.

"What can you tell me about that guy?"

Jamie blinked. "He's frustrated?"

"No." Deanna elbowed Jamie in the side. "Like what can you," she dropped her voice and glanced around to make sure they were unobserved, "*tell me about him*. With your, you know."

"Oh. With my *you know*. Right." Jamie pulled Deanna to a stop. Arthur grumbled as he waited. Jamie pursed her lips and cocked her head to listen.

"He's arguing with a woman named Kat. She found out that he was only dating her because he was bribed by a friend."

Deanna's eyes widened.

"He's trying to convince her that he actually fell for her. But he only started dating her because his friend wanted to date her sister Bianca."

"Seriously? Holy crap." Straight people were amazing.

"No, Dee, not seriously." Jamie rolled her eyes. "That's the plot to *10 Things I Hate About You*."

"Oh." Deanna deflated.

"You have got to stop watching *Teen Wolf*. You know that show's completely inaccurate, right?"

Deanna huffed to cover her embarrassment and tugged on Jamie's hand so they continued forward. So what if she had the MTV show on in the background while she worked? Those dudes were hot. And gratuitously shirtless.

"You're useless on two legs, that's what you're telling me?"

"Hey." It was Jamie's turn to be offended. "I'm not useless." She hefted the bag of fresh groceries she was carrying.

"All right, not totally useless," Deanna amended.

"I can do stuff," Jamie said defensively. "Just not, like, superhero stuff."

"Superhero lite." Deanna snickered.

"It's like…" Jamie hummed thoughtfully. "When I'm a wolf everything is heightened, and when I'm a human it's dull. Probably less dull than it is for you—"

"Thanks."

"But still less. And because I've always been this way, it's hard to say what's different for me."

"You can heal instantly. And you're strong. Fast, too," Deanna pointed out.

Jamie nodded. "I've probably got better hearing, a better sense of smell. I've never needed glasses—that might be tied into the healing thing—and I think touch might be more important to me than to other people." She gave Deanna's hand a squeeze.

"Oh yeah?" Deanna kept her voice casual as she slid her hand up to Jamie's wrist and tightened her fingers until she could feel the Jamie's pulse scramble against her fingertips.

Jamie sucked in a breath.

Deanna smirked and picked up the pace.

⌨

"So who, like, enforces your rules?"

"Mmmph?" Jamie nuzzled deeper into the pillow.

"Are there cops? Oh my god," Deanna gave a delighted laugh. "Do they have a *K-9* unit? K-9. *Canine*. Get it?"

"Wolf. *Lupine*. Do we have to do this now," Jamie's voice was slurred with sleep and muffled against the pillowcase.

"Come on, I wanna know." Deanna snuggled closer to Jamie and propped her chin against Jamie's back.

Jamie groaned, but shifted her head so that she was no longer talking directly into the bedding. "There's an assembly. We appoint people to it. They're in charge."

"An assembly?" Deanna asked, crestfallen. That didn't sound especially supernatural. Kind of boring. More like a corporation than a coven.

"GNAAW."

"What do you mean, naw? You just said—"

"No, not *naw*," Jamie mumbled. She hadn't opened her eyes and was clearly hoping Deanna would drop it so she could go back to sleep. "G.N.A.A.W. General North American Assembly of Werewolves."

"You're joking."

"I'm *sleeping*."

"Right. Okay." Deanna kissed Jamie's shoulder and felt Jamie slump, her entire body going lax as she instantly dropped off again.

GNAAW. Deanna needed to meet whomever it was that came up with the name. They clearly appreciated a good werewolf pun when they found one.

Chapter Thirteen |

CRYWOLF HAD BEEN SILENT FOR the better part of two weeks. He was quiet on the *Wolf's Run* message boards, and several of the staff and players were celebrating his absence. While the staff had done their best to shut him down almost as soon as his comments popped up, he had still managed to make such a nuisance of himself that amongst the hardcore players, and even the part-time and volunteer staff, his name was infamous.

Since the full moon was approaching, and along with it *Wolf's Run*'s monthly Moon Revel event, Deanna was taking his distance as a reprieve. She could hardly believe that it had been so easy to get rid of him—but maybe Nathan's theory had been right, and he'd seen them go to the cops. It wasn't impossible that the threat of human police had been enough to scare him away. Though she couldn't tell Nathan, Deanna suspected that it might have more to do with the werewolf laws crywolf was breaking than the human ones.

Not being able to tell Nathan was practically killing Deanna. They'd been best friends for years, and as Deanna had never been good at keeping secrets, this was torture. So far she'd managed to dodge serious conversations and was using the not entirely untrue excuse of wanting to spend time with her new live-in girlfriend to avoid hanging out with Nathan. Deanna wasn't sure how long she could keep up the ruse, but was determined not to let Jamie down. Telling someone she was a werewolf took a lot of trust, and Deanna didn't want Jamie to have misplaced it.

However, when she got bored working she rehearsed how to tell him—there was no way she could keep the secret *forever*, and Nathan's face when he found out was going to be *great*.

As for Jamie, she was happier than Deanna had ever seen her. With the exception of crywolf, and the way Jamie sprang instantly to alert whenever Deanna's buzzer or phone rang, she seemed to float through the air every evening when she came home to Deanna.

Deanna couldn't deny that the domestic bliss they'd achieved was affecting her as well. She was getting used to sleeping curled up in Jamie's arms, and that morning she'd spent five minutes staring adoringly at Jamie's toothbrush tucked into the cup beside hers on the bathroom sink. She'd been mortified when she snapped out of it, and done her best to be irritated when she'd gone to do a load of laundry, only to find that Jamie had tossed a number of her dirty clothes into Deanna's hamper. Of course, seeing Jamie's T-shirts and the tank top and underwear she slept in tangled up with Deanna's own working-from-home-yoga-pants ensemble had just made Deanna grin like an idiot as she loaded up the washing machine.

If Deanna weren't careful, she might get used to this.

Realizing that she'd been waxing romantic over the memory of doing laundry, of all things, Deanna shook herself back to alertness. She'd been skimming through the Out Of Character message boards on *Wolf's Run* while she jotted down information about that evening's Moon Revel so that she could send out a mass howl about it before her shift was over.

Whenever the full moon fell on a Friday or Saturday night—only a few times a year—the monthly Moon Revel became less a player meetup and more of a party. They changed the location for the Moon

Revels every month, which were always integral to the plot of *Wolf's Run*. The Moon Revels represented major battles for territory, and often introduced a new storyline or direction for the game. Whichever two packs had the most members show up and claim territory could compete in a scavenger hunt. Whichever pack won the Hunt won the territory.

Generally, the *Wolf's Run* admin team chose public parks or, in the winter months, a shopping mall, but this month they were holding the Moon Revel in the woods surrounding the university. They'd rented the large amphitheater buried deep in the forest, and due to the excitement surrounding the venue, the Friday night and the number of players planning to attend, Deanna knew that the admin team planned to reveal a new chapter of *Wolf's Run* after the Hunt.

Pulling up Taylor Swift's *1989* on iTunes, Deanna settled into her chair and began to compose her message to the players, letting them know what time to expect the event kickoff and the availability of parking near the venue.

She was halfway through typing the third paragraph when her music cut off. Frowning, she traced over her trackpad to pull iTunes back up, but it wouldn't respond.

"Oh, come on, you're brand new! You can't give out on me now," she complained, pressing down again to see if anything changed. When her screen went black, she yelped, jerking her hands back in case she did any more damage.

Arthur heaved himself up from where he'd been staring out the window to see what the fuss was about, and Deanna gave him an absent pat as she reached for the power button. She'd try the age-old cure of turn-it-off-and-then-on-again before she truly panicked.

"Don't touch it, Dee," a voice growled from her speakers. Deanna clamped her mouth shut; a startled scream choked off in her throat.

"What the fuck," she whispered, pulse pounding in her ears. There must be some sort of malware on her computer. Some kind of virus. She reached forward again.

"I said, don't touch it."

This time she flew back from the computer, standing up so abruptly that her chair crashed to the floor behind her and Arthur scrambled out of the way, his claws skidding on the hardwood.

Her screen flickered and then a face filled it: a wide grin stretched and distorted as a pair of orange eyes gleamed out at her.

Deanna pressed a hand against her chest as though she could control the frightened leap of her heart through sheer force of will. Her eyes flicked to the top of the screen, where the cheerful green light of her webcam winked at her. Whoever was grinning out at her from her screen—and Deanna had a pretty good idea who it might be—had taken over her webcam as well. Fuck him. If he thought some high school hacker tricks were enough to have her running scared, he had another thing coming.

Moving with deliberate calm, Deanna dropped her hand and looked dispassionately into the camera. "Let me guess," she said, "crywolf."

"Bingo." The man's grin widened. "You've been a bad girl, Dee."

Deanna snorted, rolling her eyes though she could feel her fingers tremble at her sides. "What next, are you going to tell me I need to be punished?"

The man's eyes hardened; his grin fractured into something sharp and brittle as he bared his teeth. "Careful."

"Or what?" Deanna raised an eyebrow. "You'll spam my Twitter account again? Don't you think that's getting a bit old?"

The man shook his head, tsking. "We've moved past that. I'd hoped you would realize that by now. Didn't my present teach you anything?"

"Yeah. You're shit at Photoshop."

"No one likes a bitch."

"I don't need you to like me. I need you to leave me alone."

"Not going to happen, Dee." His eerie orange eyes, so out of place on what was a relatively ordinary face, were fixed on her. He had shaggy dirty-blonde hair and a shadow of stubble on his chin. He seemed to be a few years younger than Deanna. It was hard to believe that this unremarkable man was crywolf, the person who'd caused her so much anxiety over the last months.

"Look—" Deanna changed tactics, keeping her voice soft as she picked her chair off the floor to sit in front of the laptop so they were now more or less at eye level. "I get that you're feeling insulted. I know you think *Wolf's Run* isn't... isn't respecting you." Maybe all he needed was a sympathetic ear. Maybe if she just let him talk to her he'd let it go, and get on with the rest of his life. It was a long shot, and a large part of Deanna was repulsed at the idea of sympathizing with someone who'd gone out of his way to terrorize her, but she could just shut her laptop if he got out of hand. He wasn't in the room with her, no matter what the initial shock of seeing his face made it feel like. "But it's just a game," she continued. "Everyone is only pretending. They don't mean any offense. They don't think any of this is real."

"They will." His grin returned as he rolled his shoulders back and cracked his neck. The movement pushed him back from his computer and let Deanna see that he was shirtless. She wasn't sure what she'd expected—corded muscle and hard flesh—but his skin was soft, pasty. He looked like someone who worked a boring desk job, not someone who could turn into a giant predator.

"What do you mean, they will?" Deanna's voice sharpened as she narrowed in on his last statement.

"I thought about giving you a preview. A taste." He licked his lips, and Deanna had to press her own tightly together to stop them from curling in distaste. "You're just like the rest of them, though. You didn't listen to me, even though I tried to reach out to you."

"Stalking me, that's what you call reaching out?" Deanna tried to keep a lid on her temper, but it was leaking out. Seriously, who did this guy think he was? The only thing that differentiated him from a thousand other jerks on the Internet was his eyes—and the unspoken implication there. It was easy to ignore that implication with his face in front of her, when she could see that he was nothing more than an entitled, disgusting creep.

He was breathing heavily now, his chest heaving under the sparse dusting of hair. Anger brought color to his cheeks, the red leeching the oddness from his orange eyes. Maybe he wasn't a werewolf, she thought with a sudden glimmer of triumph. Maybe she'd guessed right; he'd gone for a pair of cheap Halloween contacts and was exactly what he looked like—a mouth-breathing, unshaven, and probably unwashed troll.

"Fine," he was snarling at her, spittle flecking the camera on his end. "Fine. You can find out when they all do. With the rest of the sheep. While you're all gathered, all plump and pretty for me."

He stood up and backed away from the camera, and for the first time Deanna caught a glimpse of the room he was in.

"Gathered where?" Deanna asked, absently, hoping to keep him talking for a few more moments so she could try to find something distinguishing about the room. There was a bare light bulb hanging from the low ceiling behind him, a small window to his left. The walls were cement, the floor the same. The chair he'd been sitting in rolled, following the slant of the floor and Deanna's eyes unthinkingly tracked the movement. The chair came to a stop slightly behind crywolf at a dip in the floor where a drain was set. Around it was a dark stain, surprisingly large to be in what looked like someone's basement.

"The Moon Revel."

Deanna was still staring at the stain. The shape of it was somehow familiar, and though she'd heard what he said, she didn't quite register it. She'd seen that shape. She'd seen a pool of something liquid and almost black, stark and vivid against concrete.

Blood pooled dark underneath her, streaks of it shockingly red against a woman's pale skin.

Her blood turned ice cold, and she could feel it drain from her face. No, it wasn't—that wasn't possible. It had been Photoshop. A picture he'd found on some horrible site online. Except that she knew it wasn't.

"You…" she couldn't string her words together, couldn't pull her eyes from the shape of that awful stain. "You're a *monster*."

"And I guess that makes you the girl who cried wolf. See if anyone will believe you now." His eyes glowed when he threw back his head and showed a mouth wide and deformed. His teeth began to elongate, becoming things sharp and white and vicious. Becoming weapons.

Deanna abandoned all curiosity and slammed her laptop shut, but not before the first chilling note of a howl echoed from her speakers.

The sudden silence rang in her ears. She swallowed, pressing her clammy palms flat against her thighs, fingers digging into her own skin in the vain hope the pain would ground her. Arthur was a stiff presence at her side; a low growl rumbled from his chest.

"Shh." Deanna forced herself to move a hand and stroke the soft fur of Arthur's head. "He's gone now. He's gone." She'd told crywolf that it was just a game—that it wasn't real. She hadn't really understood, had she? Despite seeing Jamie shift in front of her, despite knowing that werewolves weren't just a fairy tale or a horror story, she hadn't quite grasped the gravity of what that had meant. He'd killed someone. And he'd sent a picture of that to Deanna. The worst part was, Deanna didn't know her name. Didn't know her face. All that was left to remember of the woman he'd murdered was the stain of her blood on a basement floor.

Bile flooded Deanna's mouth, and she shoved back from her desk. She stumbled blindly into the bathroom, knocking her shoulder against the doorway before she dropped to her knees in front of the toilet. She just managed to lift the lid and the seat before she vomited, retching violently while her fingers clung to the cold porcelain.

When she finally managed to stop, she was shaking. Her whole body was covered in a thin sheen of sweat that immediately began to cool as she slumped down against the bathmat. Her mouth tasted sour; her eyes stung with tears.

What was she doing? What made her think that this was something she could deal with? Lifting a shaking hand to wipe at her mouth,

Deanna leaned against the side of the bathtub. It was too much. It was all too much.

When she thought her legs would carry her, she pushed herself to her feet, moved back into the main room and yanked her suitcase from the storage cupboard. She crossed to her dresser, pulled out a haphazard bunch of clothes and tossed them in. She left her laptop where it was, not bothering with anything other than her cell phone and Arthur's leash as she zipped the suitcase closed and set it beside the door.

Jamie answered her phone on the first ring, alarm sharp in her voice. "Deanna."

"I thought it was a joke."

"What?"

"'My girlfriend's a werewolf.' It sounds funny, you know? It's like a joke."

"Dee, what—"

"It's not a joke, though. It's not. You're fast and you're strong and you grow fangs. Not cute fangs. Big ones. Because you're a wolf and wolves aren't prey, wolves are what hunts prey, and now he's hunting *me,* and Jamie, I don't have fangs!" Deanna could hear the hysteria in her voice. Her fingers tightened around the handle of her suitcase until they hurt. "I'm leaving. I'm sorry. I can't deal with this. I can't. He *killed her,* Jamie. I could see—" She had to swallow around the jagged lump in her throat. "I could see where he killed her."

"Who?" Deanna didn't need to see Jamie to know that she was on her feet, probably already halfway out the door of her research assistant' office.

"The girl from the picture."

"What happened?" Jamie demanded. "Where are you?"

"I'm at home. I was at home. He—he did something with my computer, took it over for a video chat." It sounded ridiculous. "The room he was in, though, it was the same room that picture was taken in, and I can't—" She broke off again, pressing her phone between her ear and shoulder as she maneuvered Arthur and her suitcase out the front door, then turned to lock it behind her.

"Deanna, breathe. Slow down and breathe and stay where you are. I'm on my way."

"No." Deanna shook her head though Jamie couldn't see it. "I can't stay here. I need to get out. I need to get away." The stairs were awkward, and she nearly dropped her phone. She was going to need two hands to get her suitcase down the stairs.

Leaning against the wall of the stairwell, she pressed a shaking hand over her eyes. "I'm sorry, Jamie. I'm really sorry. I thought I could deal with this. It didn't seem like such a big deal, you know?" She smiled humorlessly. "So you're a real bitch a couple times a month? So what? I've been accused of the same."

"Deanna." Jamie's voice was terse.

"I can't do it, though. I'm not capable of this. I mean, what *can* I do? I can't call the cops. What would I tell them? That there's a murderous rogue werewolf on the loose and he's going to attack a bunch of… of role players? At the Moon Revel tonight. That's what he said."

"I'm coming, Dee. Go back to your apartment and lock the door, and I'll be there in a few minutes, okay?"

"No. I can't—I can't stay here. It's not fun anymore." Deanna barked out a laugh and it echoed harshly in the stairwell. "I'm an idiot. I'm such an idiot."

"Please don't go."

"I have to, Jamie. I can't help you. I can't help anyone. I'm not prepared for this." Deanna insisted. One of the wheels on her suitcase was stuck on a baluster and she gave it a desperate yank, too uncoordinated to stop to free it gently. "You are though. You've got a whole pack. And your—your assembly. They'll help. They'll know what to do; they'll know how to keep everyone safe. That's their job." With one last, violent tug her suitcase came free, and she hurried down the final few stairs. "You've got this, right?"

There was a long moment of silence on the other end of the line. Deanna couldn't even hear Jamie breathing.

"Yeah, Dee. I've got this," Jamie responded finally.

"I'm sorry. I'm so sorry." Shame clogged Deanna's throat. "Just… be safe, Jamie." Before she could change her mind, and before she could let Jamie change it, Deanna ended the call and turned off her phone. If crywolf could hack into her computer, she had no illusions that her phone would be safe. And if she didn't have to ignore Jamie's calls, well then, so much the better.

She grabbed a cab to Nathan's, promising to pay double the fare when the driver looked doubtfully at Arthur. At mid-afternoon on a Friday Nathan was still at work, but she had a spare set of keys to his car and his place. He'd be pissed when he came home and realized she'd taken his car, but he'd live. And she'd call him once she got to her parents' house. She didn't know what she was going to tell him. She'd think of something.

After tossing her suitcase in the trunk and ushering Arthur into the back seat, she let herself into the driver's side and started the car. If they didn't make any stops, they should be at her parents' house in a couple of hours. Deanna didn't know what she was going to tell them, either, but she didn't let herself worry about it as she headed for the highway. She'd come up with something. She always did.

Chapter Fourteen |

DEANNA HAD THOUGHT THAT THE farther out of the city she got, the calmer she would feel. She'd been sure that the nausea in her stomach would abate, that the lump lodged in her throat and the numbness in her fingers would ease. It made sense—she was safe out of the city. Crywolf had made it fairly clear that he was upset about *Wolf's Run*, and so far the game hadn't expanded to her parents' smaller town. She'd be out of harm's way and she'd warned someone else about what he'd threatened, so the burden of all those lives wasn't hers anymore. She'd done everything she could. She hadn't asked to be a part of this, but she'd done the best she could, and now she was getting the hell out of dodge. Exactly as anyone else in her position would have done.

So she should be feeling better, right?

Deanna glanced into the rearview mirror to check on Arthur. He'd been unreasonably anxious for the first hour of their drive, moving restlessly across Nathan's upholstery and covering the dark fabric with his golden fur. He'd finally stopped pacing and now lay curled into a tight ball on the back seat. He wasn't sleeping, though; his brow was a worried furrow.

She jerked her gaze back to the highway in front of her; her palms, still damp with sweat, clamped tighter around the steering wheel. Her stomach continued to twist in uncomfortable knots, and before she could stop herself she checked the time on the dashboard. It was about half past six. The kickoff for the Moon Revel wasn't until eight, but considering the number of players who'd RSVP'd to the official Facebook event and the long hike to the amphitheater, it was likely that people had already begun to gather.

She wondered if crywolf too was already there, lurking in plain sight, looking like any one of the hundreds or thousands of players in the city.

Don't think about it, she ordered herself. If she didn't think about it she might be able to breathe around the tightness in her chest. She hadn't taken a full breath since she'd seen the bloodstain on the concrete floor. *Don't think about it*, she repeated furiously. *Don't think about it, don't think about it, don't think about it.*

Her heart picked up the rhythm, slamming against her ribs until she felt as if she were choking on its meaty pulse. Needing to distract herself from its thundering—*don't think about it, don't think about it, don't think about it*—Deanna uncurled one of her hands from the wheel and jabbed at the power button for the radio. It took three tries to hit the right button; her hand shook uncontrollably. The car filled with an electronic club mix, bass pulsed from the speakers and her eyes blurred with sudden tears.

Then Arthur was at her side, his nose pressed cold and wet against the bare skin of her neck. With a jolt, Deanna pulled her attention to the road in front of her; she'd been drifting toward the center line. She jerked the wheel, reacting on adrenaline-fueled instinct rather than knowledge, and sent them sharply toward the shoulder before she managed to slam on her brakes. The sudden stop flung Arthur forward into the back of her seat and his high-pitched yelp of pain cut through Deanna like a shard of glass.

She yanked the key from the ignition and released her seatbelt. She raced to pull open the back door and see how badly he was hurt.

"Baby, I'm so sorry," she gasped, tears falling unchecked as Arthur cautiously picked himself up and moved toward her, giving a slow wag of his tail as though to tell her he was okay.

Deanna hugged him, burying her face in his neck as she tried to fight back the sobs that shook her entire body. She felt sick again, and knew this time that it wasn't from the shock or the horror of the day, but the oily slick of guilt burning in her gut. She'd run, with her tail between her legs and without a second glance. She'd left her girlfriend alone to deal with someone who was a monster—in every sense of the word. And trying to convince herself that she'd done the right thing made her the worst sort of coward.

"I'm sorry, baby." Crouched on the side of the road with gravel digging into her knees, she was still whispering into Arthur's fur. "I'm sorry."

He nosed closer, solid and trusting, and Deanna gave one last shuddering sob, inhaling the warm scent of him. She knew what she had to do. She had probably known it the moment she'd passed the city limits and her skin had gone clammy. Giving Arthur another reassuring pat, she made sure he was settled comfortably before she got back into the car.

After flipping down the sunshade, she used the small mirror to look herself square in the eye. Her mascara hadn't fared well; her soft green eyes were circled with smudged halos. She pulled a tissue from the box Nathan kept in the glove compartment to clean up until she looked less like a raccoon. The minor cosmetic repair settled something inside her, and she herself gave a little half-smile as she recalled one of her favorite quotes: *Put on some lipstick, pour yourself a drink and pull yourself together*. Well, she couldn't pour herself a drink, but she could put on some damn lipstick.

Deanna pulled out her favorite color and applied it carefully. With her hair pulled back and her face still blotchy from tears, Deanna didn't think she'd win any beauty contests; but there was a glint of resolve in her eyes, and that more than made up for it.

Deanna eased the car from the shoulder. Checking that the way was clear, she turned them back toward the city.

It felt good to be doing something other than running.

It took another hour to get back. Deanna fought the urge to speed recklessly, but nothing would be stupider than to die in a car crash when there was a werewolf out for her blood and everyone else's. She called Jamie twice from the road, which was also stupid when she didn't have a hands-free device, but when she turned her phone back on, she found a text from Jamie saying not to worry about the Moon Revel because she'd take care of everything.

Deanna wanted desperately to catch Jamie before she went into the woods.

Jamie's phone had gone to voicemail both times.

Hey, this is Jamie. Leave a message and I'll call you back.

When Deanna turned off the highway and stopped for a red light, she grabbed her phone. She would call Nathan and see if he knew where Jamie was. She didn't think he would, but she didn't know what else to do.

Glancing down at her phone, Deanna frowned in dismay. She hit the center button again, but the screen remained stubbornly dark. She realized that she hadn't charged it before she'd fled town. The stupid battery had died, and now she didn't have a way of getting a hold of anyone.

As the light turned green, she punched the gas. She and Jamie had been planning to go to the Moon Revel around seven, as Deanna had wanted to spend time with some of her coworkers before the Hunt started at ten. The moderator team was invited to the event, of course, but they weren't responsible for any of the organization, which meant they could just mingle and have fun. They'd planned to have a couple drinks and play a few of the dorky werewolf-themed games together. It was already nearing eight and, now that she couldn't get a hold of Jamie, Deanna abandoned her plans to go back to the apartment first. She'd have to head straight for the woods and the amphitheater.

Gnawing on her bottom lip, Deanna broke her own rule and drove just a little too fast. She had no idea when crywolf planned to reveal himself, but something told her that his flair for the dramatic meant it would be when the most people were gathered in the same spot, so it would probably be right before the participants in the Hunt were announced. That meant that she had just barely two hours to get there, and the hike into the woods would take almost that long.

When she finally pulled into the parking lot, there wasn't a single free spot left. Deanna glanced at the dashboard clock. She could try to find somewhere to park on the street, but—

Okay, seriously? she asked herself. A murderous werewolf was loose among hundreds of unsuspecting people and she was worried about boxing someone in? With a quick shake of her head and a stern word to herself about getting her priorities in order, Deanna pulled in behind an expensive-looking sports car. A person who'd paid that much for their vehicle wouldn't risk damaging it by backing into Nathan's car. If she not only stole his car but also got it rear-ended, she didn't think he'd forgive her anytime soon.

She jumped out and went around the back to let out Arthur. Deanna clipped on his leash before she went to the trunk and popped it open. She didn't know what she was looking for exactly, and she knew she was too focused on simply getting to the Moon Revel rather than what she would do once she got there, but it was all she had to work with at the moment.

Nathan had a spare tire, a first aid kit, an extra blanket and a sports bag tucked into the small space. Deanna unzipped the bag, laughing happily when she realized it was his baseball equipment. An aluminum bat wasn't exactly a silver bullet, but she figured it would make a decent weapon, better than the hockey stick she would have found in a winter month.

Deanna tossed the first aid kit into the duffel bag and zipped the whole thing up, slung it over her shoulder and gathered Arthur's leash tight into her hand. She squared her shoulders, took a deep breath and followed the path into the woods.

Chapter Fifteen |

THE MOON REVEL WOULD HAVE already kicked off by now, and the dirt and gravel of the path into the woods had been tramped by hundreds of pairs of feet. Deanna knew she probably wouldn't be one of the last to arrive—there were always stragglers—but knowing that only half an hour earlier the path had been streaming with people, all loud and laughing and heading in the same direction, but was now still and silent, made the skin prickle on the back of her neck.

The farther she moved down the path, the more she became aware of the oppressive feel of the trees pressed close to the sides of the path. She'd always found their large branches, and the almost tunnel-like path through them, to be comforting; but tonight the branches, heavy-laden with leaves, only blocked the light of the setting sun. Although it wasn't late enough for the sun to have set, the heavy foliage cast the woods into an early dusk, and Deanna wished not for the first time that evening that she'd thought to charge her goddamn phone before she'd left her house. Without her phone and its flashlight app she had nothing to light the trail, and though it was still light enough to see where she was going, she knew it wouldn't stay that way much longer.

And, as soon as she'd started carrying her phone she'd stopped wearing a watch, so she had no idea how much time she had left to get to the Moon Revel.

The thought spiked her anxiety. She had no idea where Jamie was, where crywolf was, or what plan, if any, Jamie had been able to put in place. God, how could she have been so selfish as to abandon her girlfriend to deal with this on her own? It would be as if Jamie had thrown up her hands and insisted that Deanna do something about all the world's bigots because they were humans and therefore Deanna's species, and so her responsibility.

Deanna wasn't sure if she'd ever be able to get Jamie to forgive her, and knew she couldn't blame Jamie if she decided not to bother. The idea that she might have destroyed any chance of a future with the other woman made Deanna's throat tighten, and she ruthlessly dug her nails into the palm of her hand to stop another onslaught of tears. She would deal with that problem tomorrow, or whenever they'd resolved this crisis with crywolf. She needed to stay calm and focused and do whatever she could to stop crywolf from hurting anyone else.

Tamping down her anxiety, Deanna picked up her pace. She'd let Arthur off his leash, after he'd shown that he would stick close to her side and not dart off into the woods as he customarily tried to do when they took this route. He padded silently on the path beside her, his ears perked and gaze straight ahead as if he knew they were here with a purpose, and it wasn't to chase squirrels.

She had wanted to leave Arthur in the car, where he'd be safe from whatever happened at the Revel. Unless, of course, crywolf hadn't beat Deanna to the amphitheater, in which case he might recognize Arthur in the parking lot. He already knew what the dog looked like, and he'd proven that he wasn't above much when it came to scaring Deanna. The last thing she was going to do was leave Arthur trapped and defenseless. And she felt good having him at her side as they continued deeper into the forest.

The farther in they got, the more overgrown the trail became. Because of all the people who'd passed through before them, it wasn't as harrowing as it usually was. Any debris had been moved out of the way hours ago, but the path had begun to narrow until there was only just room for her and Arthur to walk side by side.

Deanna hefted the bag more securely onto her shoulder and wished that Nathan had left behind a water bottle. When they'd first started into the woods, she'd had to fight the urge to run, but she'd never be able to keep up the pace until she got there—and if she arrived exhausted and rubber-legged then she'd be of no help to anyone. So they moved at a brisk walk. They'd taken the walk all the way to the amphitheater before, and at their usual meandering pace—with plenty of time for chasing squirrels—it took them a couple hours. Deanna was counting on it taking less tonight.

Rounding another corner, Deanna felt her heart leap into her throat at the snap of a branch somewhere ahead of them. Arthur woofed quietly and his ears flattened, and they both moved forward with a little more caution, only able to relax when they rounded another curve and saw that they'd caught up to a couple heading toward the Revel. Deanna gave a strained smile and a wave as she hurried past them. The woman waved back at her happily.

Even though she knew neither of them had been crywolf—the woman obviously was not, and the man was Asian—Deanna wasn't comfortable until she was far enough down the trail that she could no longer hear them. Despite the chilling silence of the woods around her, Deanna knew that once she reached the mass of people, the thought that crywolf could be part of any group, sidling in all innocuous and human-looking, would be awful.

Though the air had cooled after sunset under the heavy canopy of trees, Deanna could feel sweat slide down her back and knew she'd long since chewed off her lipstick. Her panicked flight from the city seemed to have happened years—not just hours—ago, and the day's emotional extremes were wearing on her.

She'd managed to keep herself so focused on moving forward that she hadn't allowed herself any time to figure out what she was actually going to do once she reached the Revel, but as the woods grew darker Deanna began to catch the sound of music and people as it filtered through the trees. Shaking off the weariness that had started to settle over her, she gave in to her overriding sense of urgency. She clipped Arthur's leash back on to keep him close to her in the crowd of people and started forward at a jog.

When she was finally clear of the trees, Deanna blinked as the bright lights of the stage and the garden lights set up around the amphitheater to highlight the stairs destroyed her night vision. The stands were full of laughing, chattering people, and the large half-circle at the bottom was packed full. She shielded her eyes as she tried pick out any familiar faces. Not having any luck, she picked her way toward one of the stairways dug into the hill and made her way down.

The amphitheater was huge, easily able to fit the hundreds of people who'd shown up. With the DJ blaring music from the speakers that had been installed around the space, the lights from hundreds of camera flashes, and the odd neon costume piece, Deanna felt both blinded and deafened after the silence of the woods.

How would she find Jamie? How would she find crywolf? And, now that she was here, what would she do if she did find him? There were families here—people with their kids, people with their friends, people with their lovers—what could Deanna do to keep them safe?

"Deanna, hey!"

Deanna jolted. Her heart leapt into her throat until she recognized one of her coworkers as he made his way toward her.

"Hi, Ravi," she said with a forced smile.

"We thought we'd see you earlier," Ravi chided good-naturedly. "You almost missed the kickoff!"

"I had, um, car trouble," Deanna improvised, still scanning the crowd around them.

"Sucks. But here, let me get you a wristband. You're with the Hollow Cave Pack, right?"

Deanna focused on Ravi. "I don't need a wristband," she began, but he had already pulled one from his bag.

"Of course you do! You've gotta represent, Dee. Besides, if your pack is one of the two biggest, you won't be able to participate in the Hunt without one."

Since it would be quicker not to argue, Deanna held out her wrist and let Ravi fasten the orange wristband to it. He wished her luck, then was flagged down by some newly arriving players, waving their phones and eager to prove their pack allegiance.

At the bottom of the amphitheater, Deanna pushed through the crowd, eyes peeled for any familiar face. Many players took the Moon Revel as a cosplay opportunity. While that was usually one of Deanna's favorite aspects, and she could never get over how amazingly creative some people were, it meant now that any one of the revelers in wolf masks could be crywolf. He could be the man over there with the wolf ears and the Zorro mask, or the one with the plastic white wolf mask covering his entire face. He could be standing in the cluster of people waiting to get their face airbrushed with likenesses of their avatars. And she would never recognize him.

"Damn it, Jamie," she muttered under her breath, spinning in place to try to find a face she knew wouldn't be hidden under a mask or a layer of paint. "Where are you?"

"Dee! Hey, Dee!"

Deanna jerked around; her mouth went dry as she saw Nathan waving at her from the other side of the stage. Furious, she pushed through the crowd until she and Arthur met him.

"What are you doing here?" she hissed. Nathan rarely played *Wolf's Run*, and he hadn't ever come to an event. She hadn't warned him to stay away because she'd had no reason to think he'd come.

Nathan either didn't notice her anger or chose to ignore it. "I'm on a date," he announced cheerfully, nodding behind him where an attractive black couple stood with their arms slung around one another. The man grinned when Deanna looked over, and she did her best not to scowl at him. "Better question though is, what are you doing here?" he asked. "You take my car without so much as a by your leave, just a crappy text message about needing some time at your parents', so I assume you had another fight with your gorgeous girl." He rolled his eyes. "But then *she* shows up here without you, and now you're here." He shook his head. "Women."

"You saw Jamie?" Deanna grabbed Nathan's arm. Her fingers dug into his skin until he yelped and tried to pull free. "Where? When?"

"Yikes, calm down." Nathan shot her a concerned glance. His amusement fell away at the desperation on her face. "What's wrong?"

"You have to go, okay? It's not safe to be here."

"Deanna." Now it was Nathan's turn to grab her, and he was just as gentle as she had been. "What's going on?"

"I don't have time to explain—just tell me where Jamie is and get you and your dates out, okay?"

"Not okay," he said simply. "But stay here, I'll be right back."

"Nathan, no, wait—" Deanna began, but he was already striding away from her toward the couple. Deanna made a sharp noise of frustration and slapped a hand against the stage hard enough that her palm stung. She couldn't be worrying about Nathan *and* Jamie as well as everyone else at the Revel!

Nathan was saying something to the couple, and the woman reached out, giving Nathan's arm a quick squeeze. Both of them looked disappointed, but nodded and turned back toward one of the amphitheater's stairways. Nathan watched them go, then made his way to Deanna.

"Tell me what's happening—and hey, why do you have my baseball bag?"

"Tell me where you saw Jamie."

"Not until you tell me what's going on. I'm not kidding, Dee. Does this have anything to do with that guy?"

Deanna stared at him, fear and fury warring within her.

"I'm not leaving." Nathan crossed his arms over his chest and matched her scowl. "So you might as well just suck it up and let me in on whatever's got you so worked up."

Arthur sat still between them, alert to the movement of the crowd. Deanna wanted nothing more than to press his leash into Nathan's hand and send them home, but knew with a resigned sigh that neither of them would go.

"It's… complicated. And it's going to sound crazy, or like a joke," Deanna began, recalling with the slightest flash of amusement that she sounded just as Jamie had when she was trying to tell Deanna. "But crywolf is what he says he is. He's a werewolf." She swallowed and waited for Nathan to react. Unlike Jamie, Deanna had nothing to prove that she wasn't making this up.

Nathan stared at her and then nodded. "All right. This is serious, then."

"I…" Deanna blinked, flabbergasted. "You believe me? Just like that?"

"How long have we been friends?" Nathan raised an eyebrow. "If you believe it, and you say this is urgent, then I've got to trust you've got a good reason. You could be playing an elaborate prank on me, but I'm pretty sure that after the Prank War of '08 we got that out of our systems. Besides, Jamie doesn't look like someone who condones that sort of thing, and since she was here all worried, and now you're here all worried, I'm just going to go with it." He shrugged. "So what do we need to do?"

"Okay." Deanna reasoned that the only reason he was being so cool was that he hadn't actually seen anyone turn into a werewolf. The abstract idea was probably easier to comprehend than the bone-shifting, fur-growing reality. Speaking of which. "Where did you see Jamie?"

"Over there." Nathan pointed to the other side of the amphitheater, to the first raised section. "But it was a while ago. She asked if I knew where you were." He frowned. "Does she know about crywolf?"

"Um." Deanna bit her lip as she scanned the crowd, hoping desperately for a glimpse of Jamie. "She's one as well, actually."

"No shit," Nathan said faintly. "Does that mean she's like, an animal in the sack?" He laughed at his own joke. Deanna ignored him.

"How long ago did you see her?"

"An hour, maybe?" Nathan held up his hands uselessly. "Why don't you just call her?"

"My phone died." Deanna tried not to snap that if it was that easy, she would have done it already.

"Oh, well, use mine." Nathan pulled his phone out of his pocket. Deanna pressed her lips together and tried not to let out the scream of frustration that was building in the back of her throat.

"This is 2016, Nathan, do you really think I know her number off the top of my head?"

"Fair point," he agreed, shoving his phone back into his pants. "Okay, we find her the old-fashioned way." Crouching down, he went eye-level with Arthur. "Find Jamie, boy, find her!"

Arthur gave Nathan's face an enthusiastic lick, making Nathan grimace and Deanna choke back a laugh that was only slightly hysterical.

A flash of lights came from the stage behind her, and Deanna jumped as the speaker above them roared to life. Across the theater, the crowd surged forward toward the stage and Deanna took an instinctive step back.

"Welcome to the Moon Revel. Awoooooo!" Onstage, the local DJ and avid *Wolf's Run* player they'd hired to emcee the event threw back his head in a mock howl. As one, the crowd tipped back their heads and let loose an echo that reverberated through the night.

Deanna had thought that being pressed so close to the stage would have them at a disadvantage, but she could see all the faces turned toward the stage and lit by the lights that shone out over the crowd. Gripping Arthur's leash tight in one hand and Nathan's hand tight in the other, she swept her gaze over the faces in front of her, looking desperately for the familiar fall of dark hair over a face with a wide and agile mouth, or for a pair of haunting orange eyes.

"Thank you all for coming here tonight," the DJ continued to boom. "*Wolf's Run* is so happy to have you, and I know I'm so happy to have *Wolf's Run!*" The crowd broke into applause. The cheering and wolf whistles were deafening as people still in the stands stamped their feet. "We've got a lot planned for this full moon, and I know there's a very important announcement coming later, but first! Let's get to the good stuff." The cheering continued, and if Deanna wasn't so worried about crywolf she would have been delighted to see the hundreds of happy faces of people who'd gathered just because they liked a fun little role-playing game so much. Nearby, a man had hoisted his daughter to his shoulder so she could see the stage, and the glitter in her face paint sparkled as she grinned. Deanna went cold, knowing that crywolf was in the crowd right now and that if he had his way, that little girl wouldn't be grinning for long.

"What's the plan, Dee?" Nathan had to bend down to shout in her ear. Wordlessly, she shook her head. She wouldn't know what to do until she saw crywolf.

"The two packs with the biggest turnout tonight are the Bloodrose Pack and the Hollow Cave Pack."

The crowd went wild, yelling as the two packs stomped their feet and howled.

"We've got a great new story to start telling with you, but first—the Hunt!" The cheering reached a fever pitch, and Deanna was beginning to think she'd be deaf by the night's end. She still couldn't pick out the two faces she was searching for, and the sweep of colored lights over the faces of the crowd distorted the ones she could see. A wolf mask looked as if it were leering at her; and as she peered closer, the man lifted it off his face so he could wave it in the air, and she saw it was just a kid excited about the Hunt. Frustrated, she kept a hold of Nathan's hand and began to move forward through the crowd—maybe Jamie was up higher in the seats and out of the wash of the lights.

"We've got seven of these hidden out in the surrounding woods." Deanna turned back in time to see the DJ raise a mid-sized stuffed toy deer above his head and wave it around. A ribbon was tied around its throat. In the lights it was hard to tell, but Deanna thought it was bright red. "The first pack to bring back four of them wins. And let me tell you guys, I got a peek at what's coming up next, and trust me, you want to win!"

Deanna hadn't thought the screams could get louder, but they did. She was glad for the leash and Nathan's hand, because without them she'd clap her hands over her ears. As the DJ began to go over the rules, they continued to work their way through the crowd.

"Absolutely no physical contact between players. Come on you guys, this is a game, and if anyone bullies a deer away from anyone else their entire pack forfeits, so play nice—"

The longer the event went on without an interruption from crywolf, the more tension knotted Deanna's shoulders until now they ached with it. She shoved through a particularly dense section of the crowd and wondered if she should have called in a bomb threat. They'd have had to cancel, and none of these people would be here, gathered—as crywolf had said—like sheep. She was pretty sure false bomb threats were a felony, but she wished she had thought of it earlier. She'd use Nathan's phone to make one now, except that it was too late.

"*Jamie,*" Nathan was yelling, using his height to look over heads. "*Jamie!*"

"It's no use." Deanna's resolve was crumbling, and angry tears pricked at the corners of her eyes. "We'll never find her in this mess. God, I don't know how to stop this."

There was a momentary hush of silence as the DJ held up his hand and everyone with blue or orange wristbands tensed in readiness for the Hunt. In the sudden quiet Deanna heard, clear as anything:

"Wicked contacts, bro!"

Yanking her hand free of Nathan's, she whipped around to see a pair of ghastly orange eyes glare at her from a black wolf mask that covered half of a man's face. He was clean-shaven now, and when he saw her looking, his grin widened. Deanna felt her heart stop. She reached blindly for the bag on her shoulder, and then crywolf was swallowed up by the crowd.

"There!" She grabbed for Nathan, pointing at where crywolf had just been. Onstage, the DJ gave the go-ahead, and, with another howl, the crowd exploded toward the trees. Deanna didn't have time to decide what to do; she and Nathan and Arthur were swept up and moving toward the woods. She could just see the ears of crywolf's mask in the crowd ahead and, making sure to keep a tight hold on Arthur and Nathan, she followed.

Chapter Sixteen |

ON EITHER SIDE OF THE stage, checkpoints had been set up to ensure that the only players participating in the Hunt were members of either the Bloodrose or Hollow Cave packs, and Deanna sent a mental *thank you* to Ravi for insisting she get her wristband. She and Nathan were both part of Hollow Cave, and they were waved forward. Now that they were moving through the woods, Deanna lost track of crywolf, and she tried not to let show how much that scared her.

"Seriously, Deanna." Nathan yanked her to a stop at the side of the path. "What is your plan here? You can't—" He broke off, rubbing his eyes. "If you find him, what are you going to do? If he's actually a werewolf—I know, I know," he waved a hand as she opened her mouth to protest, "I believe you, okay? But if he's a *werewolf*, what are you going to do?"

"I don't know," Deanna snapped. "All right? I have absolutely no idea. But I can't let someone get hurt."

"We can call the cops." Nathan lowered his voice, and glanced around to make sure that no one was listening. "If we tell them that someone has a gun, that he was threatening people..."

Deanna gnawed at her lip. It wasn't the worst idea. She didn't want to get Jamie in trouble with her pack, or the assembly, for exposing werewolves to humans; but none of the people here were prepared to be attacked. They were here to play a game, to have fun, not to have to fight for their lives against something they only knew from monster movies.

"Okay," she said finally. "Let's do it."

Nathan reached for his phone just as someone burst through the trees beside them. They both jumped back, Nathan into a weird pseudo-karate stance and Deanna yanking the sports bag from her shoulder. Arthur, meanwhile, gave a bark of welcome and danced up on his back legs until Jamie gave him a pat on his head.

"You're not supposed to be here." She was angrier than Deanna had ever seen her, and Deanna had to fight a twinge of guilt.

"I couldn't just leave you," Deanna argued. "I mean, I did. But that was stupid, and selfish, and I'm sorry that—"

"Deanna." Jamie's sharp rebuke cut through Deanna's apology. "Not the time, yeah?"

"Right." Deanna pressed her lips shut.

"He went that way." Nathan gestured to the trees in front of them. "We were going to call the cops, unless you have a genius containment plan that you can put into action, like, now."

"No one is calling the cops. You two, and Arthur, need to leave. I'll take care of this."

"I'm *not* leaving—" Deanna began hotly as Nathan argued, "*How* exactly do you plan on—"

"Listen to me." Jamie's eyes were beginning to pale; the shift from whiskey-gold to cold, clear gray stole Deanna's breath. Beside her, Nathan swore, low and reverent. "This isn't your fight, and this isn't your problem. Go home."

Deanna squared her shoulders, ready to argue though Jamie wasn't saying anything that Deanna hadn't said herself earlier, when a piercing howl rent the air. Jamie froze, and Arthur began to growl.

On the path, players still headed into the woods, and Deanna heard one remark to her friend, "Wow, they have the best special effects! Allison just texted me to say she saw an actual wolf!"

"We're not leaving you," Deanna said firmly, turning back to Jamie, as Nathan nodded in agreement.

"Fine. Then you'd better keep up." Jamie turned and began to run through the forest in the direction of the howl. Nathan gave a loud whoop and followed. Deanna unclipped Arthur's leash and raced after them.

It was fully dark now, and they weren't running along the path, which was still packed with Bloodrose and Hollow Cave players. They had to run beside it, and Deanna was forced to trust her feet in the underbrush. Branches whipped past her face and tore her bare arms, and after a few minutes Deanna knew blood had been drawn in more than one place. Ahead of her, she could just keep sight of Nathan's slender body pelting through the trees; his white T-shirt was a beacon she could follow. Arthur overtook him, hot on Jamie's heels.

As her heartbeat thundered in her ears, and the sound of her ragged breathing filled the air, a second howl echoed from the woods. A chill rippled down her spine. She didn't know if it was crywolf or Jamie, and the uncertainty gave her an extra burst of speed so that she nearly caught up with Nathan, even though his longer legs ate up the ground much faster than hers.

"If we die," Nathan's panting voice carried back to her, "this is going to be an awesome way to go."

Deanna didn't have the breath to tell him to shut up, but she was surprised to find that she agreed with him. She didn't want to die, but there was a certain thrill in knowing that if she did it would be in trying to fight a murderous werewolf.

The sports bag banged heavily against her back; the aluminum bat slammed into her with every jolting move forward, and she huffed her frustration but refused to drop it. She'd have nothing but her bare hands to fight with otherwise. Nathan had scooped up a large branch and held it aloft like a sword. Deanna bared her teeth as she leapt over a fallen log. They should have looked ridiculous, the pair of them chasing after a golden retriever in the forest in the dead of night, but she thought they looked fierce.

She couldn't be sure, but she thought they were pulling away from the path. *Good*, she thought, *good to stay away from the humans*. If it was odd that she'd started thinking of herself as something other than human, she didn't have time to examine the notion.

As she began to pant, and the stitch in her side started to scream with pain at every running step, Deanna realized that Nathan was slowing down. She caught up with him just in time to burst through the trees into a small clearing.

The light of the full moon shone through the break in the trees, illuminating in stark white light the scene before them. Two crumpled bodies lay at the other edge of the clearing, and Deanna could just make out a stuffed deer with its bright red ribbon clutched in the limp hand of a teenaged girl. In the middle of the clearing, two snarling wolves, both the size of small ponies, tore at each other.

Nathan's eyes were huge in his pale face, and his hand shook before he clasped Deanna's shoulder. "Jesus. You weren't kidding."

Deanna shook her head numbly. She could recognize Jamie; the bridled gray-brown of her fur was washed out in the light of the moon but stark in contrast to the darker pelt of crywolf.

Arthur hadn't paused at the edge of the clearing as she and Nathan had, and by the time Deanna could yank her attention away from the two fighting werewolves, Arthur had jogged across the field to the two bodies and was nudging the girl.

"Come on." Deanna pushed Nathan. "I've got a first aid kit in here. I don't know if it will do much good, but if they're still alive…" She let the sentence trail off as they moved as quietly as possible around the edge of the clearing.

In the center the two wolves bit and snapped at each other, leaping together with savage jaws open wide before falling back to bristle and circle on stiff legs. Deanna had to force herself to ignore them and tune out the deadly growls as she dropped to her knees beside the two strangers.

Nathan hurried to the girl's side and, when Deanna dropped the bag, he grabbed for it and rummaged for the first aid kit. "She's still alive," he told Deanna. The pads of his fingers were slick with blood from where he'd pressed them against the side of the girl's neck to check her pulse. "I just need to stop the bleeding."

Deanna nodded, already running light hands over the body of the teenage boy to see what the damage was. His torso was a mess of blood, but as she hovered over it, not wanting to touch so much exposed flesh, his chest moved with a shallow breath and her panic eased. They were both alive, and as long as Jamie kept crywolf distracted, they would stay that way.

Nathan tore several lengths of gauze before tossing the roll to Deanna, who caught it and stared blankly at the wounds in front of her. A handful of gauze wouldn't be enough to stop the boy's bleeding. "Give me your shirt," she demanded, not looking up as she unwound a strip of gauze.

Nathan complied, handing over his T-shirt before pressing his wad of gauze over the bloody wound on the girl's collarbone. Deanna folded the shirt in half before pressing it over the boy's chest and winced as blood began to soak through the fabric at once. She'd planned to tie it to him with the gauze strip, but realized she wouldn't be able to lift him, and she wasn't sure if lifting him was a good idea considering the torn mess of his chest.

Arthur stood in front of the four of them. His chest rumbled with a low growl as he watched Jamie and crywolf. Deanna had no idea what to do next, or if there was anything more they could do.

"We have to call 911," she said to Nathan, keeping her voice down. "They need an ambulance. They need a doctor."

"I know." Nathan's eyes were grim. Blood smudged his cheek and his bare chest.

Deanna looked at the two wolves, apart now and both panting. Because of crywolf's dark pelt she couldn't tell if he was injured, but Jamie seemed to favor her right front paw, and blood gleamed wetly along her flank. She wasn't as big as crywolf, and Deanna felt like crying as Jamie lunged at him again.

Nathan had worked his phone out of his pants, and was pressing at the screen awkwardly with his left hand as he kept the right pressed to the girl's shoulder.

"Wait," Deanna stopped him. "They can't come if—we can't let them know what happened. They can't see the werewolves."

Nathan stared at her. "What do you want me to do? Wait until they bleed to death? Dee, I'm calling."

Deanna knew he was right, but she could only imagine what would happen when the paramedics came with police and they saw two deadly animals and two injured humans. She wasn't sure if Jamie could survive a gunshot wound, but she didn't want to find out.

"Jamie," she called. "You have to get out of here! You have to take him and you have to *go*."

The moment of inattention was all it took. Jamie twisted to look at Deanna and that's when he struck. Hundreds of pounds of fang and muscle slammed into the exposed line of Jamie's throat. Deanna's cry of horror was drowned out by crywolf's victorious howl as Jamie crashed to the ground and didn't get up.

With a nimble leap, crywolf jumped over her body and began to stalk across the clearing toward them.

Chapter Seventeen |

NATHAN REACHED FOR THE ROADSIDE first aid kit, pulled out a flare and lit it before he grabbed his branch and rose to his feet. His face was hard with determination, but Deanna saw him swallow uncertainly. She stood with him, the baseball bat gripped tightly in both hands. As one they moved to stand in front of the two teenagers.

Arthur crouched low before them, his muscles coiled as he readied himself to attack. *What a good dog.*

Deanna met Nathan's eyes. The red light of the flare made shadows dance wildly around them and reflected off the lenses of his glasses. She thought she should say something—*I'm sorry*, or *thank you*—but Nathan grinned, sharp and sudden, and Deanna found herself laughing at the ridiculousness of it. Both of them grinning, hands stained with blood that wasn't theirs and holding what could barely be referred to as weapons, they faced the werewolf.

"Come on, you fucker," Deanna called, widening her stance. "You don't scare me."

That was a lie, since alarm bells were ringing so loudly in her ears that she didn't think she'd be able to hear anything over the sound of them, and her skin felt tight where it was exposed to the cool night air. But when she tightened her grip around the handle of the bat, her fingers stopped shaking. She might be scared, but she was still standing.

Crywolf moved closer, his muscles rippling under the thick coat of fur. At this distance, Deanna could see the damage Jamie had done. She felt a fierce well of pride at the vicious slashes Jamie's teeth had left in crywolf's side. She couldn't see if Jamie was still breathing, but Deanna refused to believe otherwise. She knew Jamie could heal—she had seen it with her own eyes, Jamie healing instantly from the odd hickey or minor bruise—and she hoped that a more serious wound only needed more time.

Crywolf moved low to the ground. His muscles bunched as he readied himself. Arthur barked furiously, and Deanna wished with an aching fierceness that she had left him in the car.

Between one breath and the next, crywolf leapt. Deanna felt more than heard a cry of fury tear itself from her throat as she ran to meet his attack. But the attack never arrived, because just as crywolf's feet left the air something quick and pale darted from the shadow of the trees to their left and drove him to the ground. A second shape followed as quickly, and before Deanna's eyes could make sense of what she was seeing, a writhing ball of fur and fangs surged past them so that she and Nathan had to leap out of its way. Arthur was still barking, but Nathan abandoned their last stand and rushed to where his phone lay, dialing as the two new werewolves continued their vicious attack on crywolf.

Deanna dropped the bat and moved in a stumbling run across the clearing. The adrenaline that had coursed through her veins only seconds earlier seemed to have fled, and with it any remaining coordination. She fell to her knees beside Jamie.

Jamie's eyes were open as she whined softly, and when Deanna pulled her hand away from Jamie's furred side she saw that it was wet with yet more blood. Deanna wiped her hand on her thigh before cupping Jamie's large head and easing it onto her lap so she could stroke the soft fur behind Jamie's ears.

"Shh, you're okay," she soothed, a thread of concern in her voice as she tried to sound confident. "Your pack is here. They've got him, and you're going to be okay." She didn't know if the two gray wolves were a part of Jamie's pack, but she figured it was a safe assumption. She could see that one of them had pinned crywolf to the ground. Its jaws locked around the darker wolf's neck as the second wolf stepped away.

"Seriously, though," Deanna continued with a wet laugh as the second wolf seemed to move directly toward her. "I wish we'd planned this better. I mean, I want to meet your family and all, but right now I look like shit."

Jamie's tail gave a soft twitch, as if she were trying to wag it, and Deanna's heart clenched painfully.

Halfway between her and crywolf, the new wolf paused long enough to go through the odd crumpling transformation. Fur slid from its body until a person rose, naked, and continued to walk toward them.

Now Deanna could see that he was male and hastily averted her eyes. She wondered if this would be one of those weird stories she could tell her and Jamie's grandchildren one day: *I met your uncle's junk before I knew his name!*

"How is she?" the guy called as he neared. Deanna risked looking up again, careful to keep her eyes above his waist. He had the same tan skin and dark hair as Jamie, with a full beard that surrounded a generous mouth.

"I don't know." Deanna looked at Jamie, trying not to let her worry overwhelm her: Jamie's wolf eyes had gone glassy and unfocused. "He hit her so hard. She'll heal, though, right?" She couldn't keep the quaver out of her voice.

"It's likely," the man reassured her, his voice calm. He bent to run a gentle hand down Jamie's side. "She's strong and still breathing. But we need to get out of here." He looked at where the two other wolves remained locked together, the low growl of the gray one just reaching their ears. "Your friend already called the cops. We can't be here when they show up."

"No, I know." Her words were thick with tears, and Deanna tried to brush them away, forgetting that both of her hands were covered in blood until she felt it wet and thick against her face.

"You'll say it was an animal." The man forced her to meet his steady eyes. "You don't know what kind. You saw it flee into the woods as you came upon the others." He nodded to where Nathan knelt between them.

Deanna nodded, not trusting herself to speak.

The man cupped his hand firmly against the side of Jamie's neck. Something in Jamie seemed to relax at the contact, and her eyes fell shut; her great furred body was suddenly lax against Deanna. As though the touch triggered something, Jamie's limp body gave a slow shudder and, more gently than in any of the transformations Deanna had seen, sort of rolled back into Jamie's human form.

Deanna pressed a soft kiss to Jamie's forehead before the man gathered her up in his arms, lifting Jamie from the ground with an inhuman ease and then striding across the clearing toward the two wolves at its edge. The new wolf snapped at crywolf when he tried to move away and, a decidedly unkind air, herded him into the woods.

Deanna rose, watching until the group disappeared into the woods, and then she turned to help Nathan.

Chapter Eighteen |

DEANNA WASN'T SURE WHEN SHE'D finally fallen asleep. Back at her apartment, she, Nathan and Arthur were too wired to sleep. Exhaustion felt like a physical weight on Deanna's shoulders, but her concern for Jamie overwhelmed anything else.

The evening didn't feel real. If it hadn't been for their bloodstained clothes, Deanna might have thought that she and Nathan had ingested a powerful hallucinogen and gone on a terrible trip. Nathan had had a worse time than she had—after all, Deanna'd had time to get used to the idea of werewolves before she'd seen the damage they could do. Nathan had found everything out in a single evening, and had spent the few hours after they'd returned to Deanna's in a state of hoarse shock before he finally fell asleep.

He'd stopped talking—the rasp of his words had dried up, and Deanna saw his head nod back against the couch; he'd been asleep before he finished his sentence. Deanna gathered up their wet towels and hung them to dry. Then she curled up in the armchair and worried uselessly at the corner of a throw pillow until she drifted off as well.

It wasn't until she heard the gentle knock at her front door that she woke up; her stiff body protested frantically as she shot off the chair.

Nathan and Arthur were both curled up on the couch. Nathan's arm was tucked firmly around Arthur's middle, and Arthur merely gave a slow wag of his tail as the knock sounded again.

Deanna pushed her disheveled curls from her face and crossed the room. She carefully checked the peephole. Seeing Jamie's pale face through the small window, Deanna wasn't sure what to expect once she opened the door, but the bone-crushing hug Jamie enveloped her in left her weak-kneed with relief.

"You're alive," she said, her voice muffled against Jamie's collarbone. She felt Jamie nod above her, and Deanna hitched her arms tighter around Jamie's ribs.

"How are you?" Jamie pulled back, cupping her hand around Deanna's cheek so she could tilt Deanna's head up.

"I'm okay," Deanna answered. Her neck hurt from the awkward position she'd slept in, and her calves were so sore from their breakneck run through the woods that every step was agony. She had an embarrassing number of scratches down her arms, and one along her cheek that Jamie was looking at with worried eyes, but otherwise, she was good. She *felt* good.

"You shouldn't have come back." Now that she had established that Deanna was alive and well, Jamie's anger from the previous night returned. "That was stupid."

"Maybe it was," Deanna agreed. "But I'd do it again."

"So would I." Deanna hadn't heard him move, but she felt Nathan's solid presence at her back. "We saved those kids' lives."

"That's not the point—" Jamie began hotly, but Nathan interrupted her with an exaggerated sigh.

"That's exactly the point. We helped. And we were badass. I mean, did you see Dee with that baseball bat?"

Despite herself, Jamie found her lips curling in a grin. "My cousin Cole said you two looked like idiots."

"Well, Cole can bite me," Nathan said, affronted. "We were hardcore. And while I appreciate him and whoever else coming in at the last minute to save the day—which, really, flair for the dramatic much?—I think we'd have given crywolf a thing or two to think about."

"Yeah, right before he ate you," Jamie rolled her eyes, but the heat of her anger had dissipated.

"What did you do to him?" Deanna caught her bottom lip in her teeth, unsure if she wanted to know the answer but needing to ask.

"They didn't kill him." Jamie's tone implied that she didn't agree with that course of action. "But he won't be allowed to hurt anyone again."

Deanna smiled. "That's good."

She wasn't sure how she'd have felt if Jamie's pack had killed crywolf. Not that she didn't believe he deserved it, and not that it wouldn't have made her think he'd paid for killing the other woman, but she didn't like the thought of Jamie falling to his level. They were better than crywolf, and they had proved that last night. After all, none of them—well, maybe Nathan, but only because he didn't understand what he was getting involved in—had thought they'd be able to take down crywolf on their own. They'd known going in that they might not come back out, but they'd gone in anyway. With that thought, Deanna realized something, and with a sharp shock of fury whirled on Jamie.

"Wait, you knew they were coming, right? When you showed up at the Moon Revel, you knew your pack would come?"

The guilty look on Jamie's face told her all she needed to know, and with a wordless sound of anger Deanna gave Jamie a solid punch on her shoulder. Jamie, perhaps predictably, didn't so much as wince.

"You stupid, self-sacrificing, moron!" Deanna punctuated her words with punches until Nathan caught her hand and pulled her back.

"She didn't do anything we didn't," he pointed out, far too reasonably for Deanna's comfort. "She was at least playing in the same league as crywolf—we had no business being there, Dee, and you know it. So don't get mad at Jamie for doing exactly the same thing we did."

Deanna narrowed her eyes but shut her mouth, knowing he was right but still unhappy about what Jamie had done, which, she decided with a sigh, was probably exactly how Jamie was feeling about her.

"Anyway," Nathan yawned, "Thank you for the couch. And thank you," he crouched to give Arthur a solid rub, "for the cuddle. But I want to get back to my own place and my own bed." Rising, he pulled Deanna close to press a soft kiss to her temple, and, to Jamie's flustered pleasure, gave her one as well.

"Get some sleep, some *real* sleep," he told them. "The 'talk' or whatever can wait."

"Thank you, Nathan," Jamie said dryly, closing the door behind him before she turned back to Deanna with her hand still on the knob. A question hung unspoken.

Deanna glanced at the clock on her wall. She and Nathan had gotten back to her place well into the early hours of the morning, and though it was now nearing noon, she hadn't slept well enough to make up for the night they'd had. A small part of her wanted to point out to Jamie that it was awfully confident of her to assume Deanna would ask her to stay, but a larger part wanted nothing more in the entire world than to curl up with Jamie, warm and safe in her arms.

"All right," she agreed. "I'll have to take Arthur out first though."

Jamie shook her head. "Let me take him."

As though he'd understood the conversation, Arthur leaned his side into Jamie, and sighed happily when she dropped a hand to scratch behind his ears.

Deanna raised her hands in defeat and stepped back to let Jamie and Arthur through the door. When it closed, she locked it and then stood in the small entryway of her small apartment.

As much as she loved Arthur, having him meant that she was rarely alone. The emptiness of the apartment was soothing in a way Deanna hadn't realized she needed; after the insanity that the last few days had been, the stillness was a balm. In the bathroom, she rinsed her face with cool water, washed the sleep from her eyes and touched the scrape on her cheek delicately. It was long, but shallow, and Deanna figured it would heal in a matter of days.

Then she began to pull the cushions from the couch, setting them to the side so that she could unfurl the mattress. The sight of her bed made her aware of the exhaustion that had settled into her bones. It was hard to believe that less than twenty-four hours had passed since crywolf had appeared on her computer screen. So much had happened since then that Deanna could have sworn it had been days.

After pulling her pillows and comforter from the cupboard, Deanna made up the bed and tidied the room. As she put the dishes from last night in the sink she heard Jamie's key in the lock, and came out of the kitchen to meet her and Arthur.

Arthur seemed to feel the same level of exhaustion as the rest of them because, with a slow wag of his tail for Deanna, he headed straight for his bed, curled up into a tight ball and groaned heavily with contentment before he closed his eyes and immediately dozed off.

Deanna held out her hand to Jamie, and with a smile Jamie took it, slotting her fingers between Deanna's. Deanna drew Jamie close and let out a shuddering sigh when Jamie simply held her. There was none of the forceful urgency of their last hug, and Deanna pressed her face into Jamie's neck, breathing in the soap-clean scent of her. Jamie's chest moved slowly and steadily and Deanna felt her own breathing fall into the same rhythm.

Deanna knew Nathan had chided them about having a talk, but standing in the middle of her apartment with Jamie's arms around her, Deanna couldn't think of anything that needed to be said. They'd both been stupid, and reckless, and somehow, miraculously, they had both survived. Though they could hash out their various mistakes later on, Deanna thought they probably wouldn't.

"Come on." Deanna pulled away, but kept her hand in Jamie's as she made her way toward the bed. Jamie paused at the edge to slip off her jeans, and Deanna pulled off her clothes. She crawled naked and comfortable into the bed as Jamie slid under the covers in her tank top and underwear.

When Jamie settled back against the pillows, Deanna leaned down, her hair curtaining them both as she found Jamie's lips with hers. The kiss was warm and sweet, a gentle affirmation of happiness and trust, and when Deanna settled down to curl around Jamie, she knew there was no place she'd rather be.

Chapter Nineteen |

DEANNA PUSHED OPEN THE DOOR to Jamie's apartment with her shoulder. She was glad no one had closed it tightly when she'd gone downstairs to bring up more wine glasses. Though Jamie's apartment was much bigger than hers, the sight and sound of over a dozen people, including two small children and one golden retriever, made it feel almost as small.

"Let me help." One of Jamie's cousins pushed herself out of the fray and took several of the delicate glasses. "You should have said something; one of us would have come down with you," she reproached gruffly.

"It was really no trouble," Deanna assured her, winding her way through to the kitchen. Kiara set the glasses on the counter before she leaned back against it with a smirk.

"You needed to escape the madness for a minute, didn't you?"

Deanna laughed, glancing past the bar to where Jamie's family— Jamie's pack—sat, and stood, and in the case of one of the kids rolled happily beside Arthur on the floor in the living room. Jamie had been apologetic when she told Deanna about their impending arrival, explaining that it wouldn't be her entire family, but still a number of them. She'd told Deanna that she didn't expect her to meet all of them, though Jamie would like it if they could have dinner with her parents.

Deanna had tried not to feel offended that Jamie had thought she'd want to do anything other than meet as many of Jamie's relatives as possible, reminding herself that her intelligent, gorgeous, turns-into-a-wolf-on-occasion girlfriend was also still an introvert; and that, far more than the werewolf thing, required understanding and accommodation from an extrovert.

"Absolutely not," Deanna said with a grin, opening the fridge to grab one of the bottles of rosé she'd stashed. "I'm just trying to get all of you—the adults, anyway—as drunk as possible so you'll be sure to like me."

"I'd say that's not necessary, but I won't turn down a drink." Kiara took one of the glasses and held it out so Deanna could pour.

Deanna poured herself a glass as well and snagged a tortilla chip from the bowl on the kitchen table. She'd spent most of the day helping Jamie get ready for her visiting family, and the jalapeño dip was Nathan's recipe.

"I wanted to say thank you again," Deanna said. "You and Cole saved our asses." She gestured at the living room, where Nathan perched on the arm of the couch beside Jamie's father. He gestured wildly as he explained the premise of *Wolf's Run*.

Kiara's lips thinned into a hard line. "He was one of us. I'm only sorry we didn't get him sooner."

In, well, *person*, Kiara didn't much resemble the sleek gray wolf who had burst from the woods with her brother to come to their rescue. She had the same dark hair as her brother and Jamie, cropped to the shoulder with a sharp line of bangs above her eyes. She and Cole were both shorter than Jamie, but while Cole was solid with muscle, Kiara was downright tiny. It would have been easy to dismiss her, save for her eyes, which were honey-gold and startlingly fierce. If Jamie was right, Kiara was in line to be the pack's next alpha. Deanna didn't want to play favorites with Jamie's relatives, but Kiara might be hers.

"Though," Kiara added, "Cole might be regretting saving your friend."

Deanna looked back into the living room to see Nathan on his feet, his outstretched arms clearly attempting to demonstrate what he had taken to calling his "last stand" with the tree branch and the flare as they'd faced down crywolf. Standing in the corner of the room, the second small child perched gleefully on his shoulders, Cole watched the re-enactment with a raised eyebrow. Deanna hid her grin with her wine glass. To his credit, Nathan had faithfully refrained from telling anyone else about their heroics. Well, the part where they came across the two teenagers and called 911, yes, but he'd been more than circumspect about the werewolf bit. Deanna wouldn't deny him the opportunity to brag among people who were already in the know.

"He has that effect on people," Deanna said cheerfully. She could understand Cole's exasperation—the way Nathan was telling the story, you'd think he'd singlehandedly saved the entire human race without breaking a sweat. The part she knew Nathan was careful not to share was that he still woke up in a cold sweat in the middle of the night, dreaming of blood on his hands and an advancing pair of orange eyes.

Deanna spent more nights at Jamie's than not, now. When she woke up scared and shaking, she had someone to wrap long arms around her. As though Jamie could tell Deanna was thinking about her, she looked up from where she'd been talking to Michael, her uncle and the pack's alpha, and smiled. Deanna smiled back. The lightness in her chest made her think she might float into the air at any second.

Kiara saw the look on Deanna's face. "Any awkward werewolf questions you can't ask Jamie that you want to get out of the way?"

"What?" Deanna turned back to Kiara, puzzled. "Should I have some?"

Kiara shrugged. "You know, 'Will we have puppies?' That's what her dad asked her mom. No joke."

Deanna's jaw dropped, and before she could stop herself she looked at Erica, who had her family's whiskey-gold eyes and was setting up an elaborate-looking board game with her brother Trevor.

"Well," Deanna began carefully, "I don't think that's something Jamie and I need to worry about right now…"

"Good, because Erica and Lowell definitely had puppies."

Deanna could feel her eyes go wide, because she knew— thought she knew— Jamie would have mentioned that, right?

Kiara broke into a laugh that, compared to her usual serious expression, was like the sun coming out from behind the clouds. "I'm sorry, oh god, your face. Lowell likes dogs. So, they had puppies. But Jamie was never a puppy."

Deanna knocked back the rest of her wine, unable to formulate an appropriate response.

"Don't worry." Kiara patted her on the arm. "You're fitting right in. Now go," she ordered with a gesture toward the living room. "Uncle Trevor's about to try to find people to play with, and if you volunteer you'll have saved me from having to play. Consider us even."

Deanna gave an affable shrug. Surely it wouldn't be that bad?

"IF I NEVER SEE ANOTHER pair of dice again, it will be too soon," Deanna swore, holding out a garbage bag as Jamie emptied the last remaining veggie tray into it.

Nathan, gathering glasses, snorted in amusement. "I think you're just bitter because Malarth couldn't make it through the White Pine Forest without rolling at least a nine and having both the Harp of Glory and the Flowering Spring cards."

"I'm not bitter," Deanna argued. "I'm exhausted. And I can't believe you not only understood that game, but won."

"It's great." Jamie was even more enthusiastic about Nathan's win than he was. "You're Uncle Trevor's new best friend, and that means I can just send you to things in my stead."

"I don't see how that's fair," Cole pointed out affably. "You're not dating *him*."

"No. But it's close enough. He's practically Deanna's brother, so," she said as she winked at Nathan, "it's like sending an in-law."

"I still don't see why you had to have both cards," Cole sighed under his breath, loading the plates into the dishwasher. "Or who let Uncle Trevor in the door with a board game."

Deanna had to stop herself from humming out loud as she moved through the room and tossed napkins and paper plates into her garbage bag. It was well past midnight and Jamie's family had left half an hour ago. Nathan and Cole had stayed behind to help clean, and Deanna thought that the evening had gone very well. Both of Jamie's parents were kind and welcoming, and with Kiara as her self-appointed, if prickly, ally, Deanna had had an easy time connecting with the rest of Jamie's family.

When they left, Michael had hugged her close and then, as he was pulling away, pressed his hand to the side of her neck. Deanna frowned. The gesture was oddly familiar, and it wasn't until she'd begun to tidy that she realized he'd done what Cole had to Jamie when she was injured in the woods. Deanna wasn't sure of the significance of the gesture, but found herself oddly touched. She knew enough about wolves—actual wolves—to know that necks and throats were significant when they interacted, and hoped that whatever the touch had meant to this pack, she wouldn't let them down.

Nathan dropped the last of the wine glasses in the sink and stretched, not bothering to hide the way he watched Cole's ass as he leaned down to add another plate to the dishwasher.

Catching Deanna watching him, Nathan flashed a cheeky grin. Deanna rolled her eyes, suspecting that if Cole had caught him looking, Nathan would have been in for a stern word or two. She hoped the next time Cole came to visit that it would happen. Nathan needed someone to call him out on occasion. It was good for his overdeveloped ego.

"Thank you for hosting, and for inviting me." Nathan pulled his attention away from Cole's butt to give Jamie a quick hug. "I'd better get back home, though. They're releasing *Mirror's Edge Catalyst* tomorrow, and I want to be up early to start playing."

Jamie gave him a tight squeeze. "Thank you for coming," she said, and Deanna had to stop herself from cooing with delight—she'd never thought that her best friend and her girlfriend *wouldn't* get along, but the fact that they were friends made her impossibly happy.

"I'll walk out with you." Cole emerged from the kitchen to give Deanna's shoulder a squeeze and wave to Jamie as he followed Nathan to the door.

"You want a ride to the hotel?" Nathan offered, all innocence save for the wicked gleam in his eye. Deanna muffled a snort with her hand, but by the side-eye Jamie treated her to, didn't think she'd done the best job.

"Sure." Cole ignored them and followed Nathan out. As the door closed behind them, Deanna pumped a fist into the air and gave a silent "*Yes!*"

"Oh, please," Jamie said. "You don't really think…?"

Deanna laughed. "I think I can't wait to see what happens." She crossed the living room and wrapped her arms around Jamie, marveling at the solidity of her. Though it had been weeks, Deanna still couldn't fathom how quickly Jamie had healed. The night of the Moon Revel, Deanna had been sure Jamie was mortally wounded. In Deanna's nightmares, the furred head she lifted into her lap was entirely still, and the blood on her hands was cold.

Jamie stroked Deanna's hair, as if she could sense the direction of Deanna's thoughts. "It's over, you know," she said. "He's gone, and those kids are fine—thanks to you and Nathan—and *Wolf's Run* is doing as well as ever."

It was true. If anything, the game had surged in popularity after the news broke that two of its players had been attacked by a wolf—a thing that hadn't happened in the last decade in Canada. Deanna wouldn't have imagined that something so horrific could cause people to want to play the game, but apparently it had added a verisimilitude that attracted new players like flies. The teenagers, both on their way to recovery, had each recounted their story of being stalked by a giant wolf to any news outlet and blogger that would listen, and were enjoying their newfound popularity as survivors of a werewolf attack. Deanna couldn't decide if it was painfully ironic or just plain hilarious that they were capitalizing so easily on what had been done to them, but she wished them all the best. Last she'd heard, the girl was in discussions with a TV producer to tell the story of a young girl, attacked in the woods and bitten by a wolf, who later discovers she has gained unnatural powers. Deanna hoped she would be able to add it to her roster of TV shows next summer.

"I know," Deanna answered belatedly. "I still can't believe we're all okay. I thought…" she let her words trail off. They'd had this conversation more than once over the past weeks, and Deanna was getting sick of it. But she couldn't help returning to it. She needed to poke at it, as if it were a fresh bruise and she wanted to be sure it was healing.

"I'm not that easy to get rid of," Jamie promised.

It seemed, incredulously, that crywolf had been. Well, not easy, Deanna amended. But once Jamie's family had arrived, the entire thing had suddenly no longer been Deanna's problem. After having to deal with crywolf on her own for months, the lack of him in her life was startling. There were still annoyed game players, and Internet trolls who'd send her rude tweets, but she no longer had to logon to Twitter with an impending sense of dread.

Deanna deliberately hadn't asked what they had done with him. That might be cowardly, but she didn't care. She didn't want to spend another minute thinking about him—which, she realized ruefully, was exactly what she was doing.

"So I see now why your place is so big," she said as she moved away to turn on the dishwasher. "And you've got how many more pack members?"

Jamie scrubbed a hand over her face. "So many. And Andrew is getting married next year, so you'll meet them all at the wedding, if not sooner."

"Why, Jamie," Deanna pressed a hand to her chest, affecting a tone of demure shock, though she couldn't keep the sparkle from her eyes. "Are you making plans with me over a year in advance?"

Jamie paused where she was tying the final garbage bag closed; a flush crawled over her cheeks. "I, um," she stammered, "I don't mean to—I know it's only been... I—" She broke off, and only when she looked up and caught Deanna's eye did she realize Deanna was teasing.

"You're not as cute as you think you are," she admonished, setting the bag down with the others.

"Oh, I think I am." Deanna gave her most winning smile. "And you love it. You love me."

"Yeah, I do."

Deanna's breath caught; her heart did an odd, tumbling fall. She hadn't expected Jamie's careful, measured response. Hadn't expected to see the quiet certainty in Jamie's eyes as she crossed the kitchen and slid her arms around Deanna's waist.

Jamie brought her head down and brushed her lips over Deanna's. "I love you," she said, the words no more than a breath of air.

Deanna reached up to cup Jamie's face in her hands, tilting her head back so that she could look Jamie full in the face. "Say it again," she demanded.

"I love you," Jamie repeated, eyes twinkling good-naturedly. "Despite your terrible sense of humor. I assume this means you'll be my date to the wedding?"

"I have a hilarious sense of humor," Deanna corrected absently, pulling Jamie's head back down so that she could press her lips against Jamie's. "And yes," she said against Jamie's mouth, "I'll be your date."

There was a cough from behind them, and they sprang apart. Deanna couldn't quite meet Jamie's dad's eye as he handed Deanna a wine glass Nathan had missed, his lips quirking in a smile.

"Hey, Dad," Jamie shoved her hands into her pockets, looking adorably like a teenager as she tried to pretend she hadn't just been caught making out with her girlfriend—never mind that she was a fully-grown adult in her own apartment. "Are you and Mom settled in the bedroom?"

"We are," Lowell said, stepping around the bags of garbage to take a bottle of water out of the fridge. "I don't think your mother's been this drunk since your Aunt Daisy's sixtieth. She's out like a light, but I imagine she'll want this when she wakes up." He lifted the bottle in a mini-salute. "You're lucky you got my iron constitution," he told Jamie. If Jamie's dark hair and brown eyes came from her mother's side of the family, her height was all her father's. Lowell was tall, but, like Jamie, his size was disarmed by the gentle way he carried himself, as though he was aware of how his size could be misinterpreted and was careful not to intimidate.

"I think my inability to get drunk might have more to do with the whole werewolf thing, but yeah, sure, Dad." Jamie rolled her eyes, and Deanna muffled a laugh.

"Now, I'm sure you don't want this garbage sitting here all night." Lowell nudged the closest plastic bag with his toe. "Why don't you and Deanna take them out? I'm going to join your mother, and the rest of the cleanup can wait until tomorrow."

"Oh," Jamie looked surprised, blinking down at the bags. "Yeah? I guess we could do that." She glanced at Deanna and gave a confused shrug.

"Well, that's settled then. Take your time." Lowell gazed absently out the window, though there was a gleam in his hazel eyes that Deanna thought she recognized. "It's a beautiful night. And I won't wait up for you." He turned and met Deanna's eyes, giving her a slow wink.

"All right, if you're sure." Jamie still sounded puzzled, but, game as always, she had hefted the two heaviest bags, leaving the lighter one for Deanna.

"See you in the morning." With a perfectly straight face, he wandered out of the kitchen as silently as he'd come in. Deanna wondered if it would be awkward if she told Jamie that she had a crush on her dad.

"Sorry," Jamie said once they were out in the hall, Arthur leading the way, "I don't know what that was all about."

"You're kidding me, right?" Deanna raised an eyebrow. "Your dad just told us to go have sex."

Her mouth falling open, Jamie stopped dead in the middle of the hallway. "He what?"

"Sorry," Deanna said around a laugh, continuing toward the stairs. "He wasn't exactly subtle. All that 'I won't wait up' business? Besides, you didn't really plan to spend the night on your couch, did you?"

Deanna had been surprised when Jamie mentioned that her parents would be staying with her, but hadn't asked to sleep at Deanna's for the duration. Deanna had figured Jamie just assumed that would be the case, but when she didn't bring it up, Deanna wondered if Jamie's parents wouldn't have been okay with it, and so she hadn't brought it up either.

Clearly, she thought with an amused grin, they would be more than okay with it.

Jamie finally caught up with Deanna, and was apparently over her shock because she began to hustle Deanna down the stairs. Deanna shook with suppressed laughter, but managed to keep a straight face. The last week had been unusually busy—Jamie had a research ethics submission due, and since none of her family had visited her in Vancouver before, she'd scrambled to have her place perfect. Now that *Wolf's Run* had become the city's top-selling app, Deanna had been swamped at work. The number of new players meant almost twice as many moderation problems as usual. They'd still managed to see each other a few times, but it had been days since they'd managed a proper sleepover, and Nathan had already sent Deanna ominous texts about "lesbian bed death," which he swore was a legitimate threat and that he had ample documentation at the library to confirm its existence.

Nathan was, of course, full of shit, and Deanna suspected the "ample documentation" was nothing more than all six seasons of the *L-Word*, but Deanna wasn't going to pass up the opportunity to get her sexy werewolf girlfriend in the sack.

After tossing the garbage bags in the bin, with Deanna holding her nose and making Jamie lift the lid for her, they gave Arthur a quick walk around the block. Lowell had been right, it was a beautiful night, and Deanna tucked her arm into Jamie's as they strolled through the cooling air. It was oddly domestic, and Deanna felt a warm glow settle in her stomach as she realized that this time next year they both planned to be doing the same thing.

Once they were back inside, they made their way to Deanna's floor. Arthur flopped onto his dog bed.

In preparation to meet Jamie's parents and various extended family members, Deanna had bought three different dresses. Before going to Jamie's she'd tried on all three many times, then dived into her closet and tried on another half-dozen dresses before she settled on the first dress she'd found at the store. After her frantic rush to look as cute as possible, she hadn't had time to tidy, so the sofa bed was pulled out and strewn with her discarded clothes.

"Sorry," Deanna said, as she began to gather them up, "if I don't hang them up now they'll be wrinkled forever."

Jamie shook her head knowingly and gave Deanna a hand, passing her the dresses so that Deanna could hang them in the tiny wardrobe in the bathroom.

"You know," Jamie said, handing Deanna a pair of nylons, "this place is really small."

Deanna glanced around. She was hanging her clothes in a closet in her bathroom, so yeah, it was a small apartment. She shrugged. "It's not so bad once you get used to it."

Jamie sank onto the unmade bed and toyed with the comforter. "You ever think of moving?"

Deanna reached behind her back to get at the zipper on her dress. "Maybe when I first got here? But, I mean, why would I?" She fumbled with the clasp; the hook was at just the wrong angle. "My girlfriend lives in the same building. I'd be stupid to look anywhere else." Jamie was off the bed before Deanna could ask for help. Her fingers brushed the bare skin of Deanna's back.

The simple touch made Deanna shiver, and she stilled as Jamie slid the zipper down. Jamie brought her hands up to the straps and pushed them down Deanna's arms, so the dress fell in a puddle at Deanna's feet. A half-smile on her face, and her skin already hyper-aware of the heat from Jamie's still-clothed body, Deanna turned around. Gently, she toyed with the short hair at the back of Jamie's neck.

Jamie looked nervous, and Deanna rose up on her toes to press a kiss to the corner of her mouth. Jamie melted into it, her lips parted against Deanna's and she gave a soft sigh that pulled the tension from her body.

"I don't mean to push," Jamie murmured. She pulled back so that she could nip at Deanna's earlobe. "Because I know it might be a lot for one day." She slid her lips lower, drifting them soft and warm against the delicate skin of Deanna's neck so that Deanna arched back, confident that Jamie would and could hold her up as her legs turned to rubber. "But, if you wanted more space, you could move in with me."

It took Deanna a moment to focus on what Jamie was saying, since she was moving a hand up Deanna's thigh and her mouth was still pressed to Deanna's neck, but when the words sank in, she scowled and wriggled free of Jamie's hands, only just managing to catch herself on the counter as she tripped over her dress.

"Seriously?" she asked, crossing her arms over her chest in mock dismay. "If I want more *space*?"

Jamie winced and rubbed her hand over the back of her neck. "It is small," she pointed out again.

"Yeah, I know it's small." Deanna was trying very hard not to roll her eyes. "But do you want me—and Arthur—to move in because my place is small, or because you want to live with us?"

Jamie blew out a breath and visibly steeled herself. "I'd like you, both of you, to move in. If you'd like. Or—we don't have to stay here. We could find somewhere else, if you want. I don't care. It's just that this place is really small, and I don't know what we'd do with my couch, and—" Deanna interrupted her monologue with a kiss, her hands grasping the collar of Jamie's shirt as she dragged the taller woman down to her level.

When Jamie finally managed to pull back she was breathless and grinning. "I take it that's a yes?"

"That is very much a yes. And I think I know exactly how we can celebrate."

"Ice cream and Netflix?" Jamie suggested, as her fingers began to unfasten the buttons on her shirt.

"Ha, ha," Deanna deadpanned. "I think I'm rubbing off on you."

"Not yet, but you will be."

The terrible pun left Deanna speechless and, as Jamie tossed her shirt to the floor and lifted Deanna over her shoulder to take her into the living room, Deanna couldn't do anything but bury her head against Jamie's shoulder blade and laugh with the cheesy absurdity of it all.

The mattress creaked when Jamie dropped her gently onto it, and as Jamie stood back to work her jeans down over her hips Deanna lay back to do the same with her underwear. "You know the only reason I am moving in with you is because of your bed, right?" she asked, tossing her panties to the floor before she sat up to unclasp her bra.

"I know." Jamie kicked her underwear to the side and crawled over the mattress to Deanna. Her hand came up to cup Deanna's breast. "I'll take what I can get," she said as she rubbed her thumb over Deanna's nipple, watching with heavy-lidded eyes while the sensitive flesh hardened. Deanna gasped when Jamie bent her head to slide her tongue over its peak; the wet drag tightened things low in her body.

Jamie slid her leg between Deanna's and rocked against her as she drew Deanna's nipple into her mouth.

Deanna reached for Jamie and tangled her fingers in her thick hair as she pressed herself closer, arching up into Jamie's mouth until she felt the sharp edge of teeth close over her breast. Deanna's lips parted on a moan when Jamie pressed her thigh more urgently against her, and when Jamie brought a hand up to slide over Deanna's open mouth, Deanna caught her wrist, holding Jamie in place as she sucked Jamie's thumb into her mouth. Jamie shuddered, her pupils blown wide as Deanna stroked the pad of Jamie's thumb with her tongue.

"God, your mouth," Jamie groaned, her free hand digging into Deanna's hips as she abandoned rubbing Deanna's clit and focused on grinding against Deanna's leg. "It's ridiculous."

Deanna gave another swirl of her tongue before pulling off Jamie's thumb. When she spoke, her voice was husky. "*My* mouth? Have I ever told you how many fantasies I had about yours?"

Jamie stilled with a confused look on her face.

Though they were well past the point where Deanna should feel embarrassed, she could feel her cheeks turn pink as she shifted, moving up until the two of them were face to face. "Your mouth," she said, as she traced Jamie's lower lip with her finger, "I wanted your mouth all over me. You'd smile at me and my heart would stop. It's so wide, and your lips looked so soft."

Jamie gave a low laugh. She bent until her mouth was a breath away from Deanna's. "Do you know why?" she asked, her head tilted as she met Deanna's eyes.

"Why?" Deanna's eyes dropped to Jamie's lips.

"Because they're all the better to kiss you with, my dear." Jamie's teeth flashed as she grinned, and before Deanna could decide if she wanted to laugh or groan, Jamie made good on her promise, easing her lips lightly against Deanna's until Deanna's mouth parted on a soft sigh and Jamie slid her tongue between them.

Deanna let Jamie push her back against the bed. She bit back a whimper when Jamie moved from her mouth to graze the side of Deanna's neck with her lips. It only took Deanna a moment to realize that Jamie intended to fulfill Deanna's fantasy, because the way Jamie's parted lips dragged over the suddenly sensitive skin of Deanna's shoulder made Deanna keenly aware of the wetness between her legs.

"Can't we save that for another time?" Deanna pleaded when Jamie moved lower, her movements agonizingly slow as the press of those soft lips along the underside of Deanna's breast made her writhe. The slow burn Jamie's mouth ignited with every touch made Deanna hungry for more, and when Jamie ignored her, kissing her way across Deanna's soft stomach, Deanna had to bite back a strangled curse.

By the time Jamie had made it down one of Deanna's legs and was well on her way up the second, Deanna was nearly mindless with need. Jamie had been careful to avoid putting her mouth where Deanna wanted it most, and at the first moist breath against her damp curls Deanna made a noise that was close to a sob.

"Please," she begged, hips arching toward Jamie where she lay between Deanna's sprawled legs with her arms curled around Deanna's thighs to keep her pinned to the mattress. For a moment she didn't think Jamie would relent, was sure she'd continue to tease until Deanna imploded with the pent-up arousal. In Jamie's position, Deanna would have had a hard time not seeing how far she could push until Jamie completely broke.

Luckily for her, Jamie took pity and leaned forward, closing her mouth around Deanna's hot flesh. She didn't move softly or gently as she had everywhere else on Deanna's body, and the sudden sensation of Jamie's tongue laving intently at Deanna's clit when she'd ignored it for what seemed like hours had Deanna rigid, every muscle in her body clenching as she came in a dizzying rush.

When Deanna sagged back against the bed, her eyes were open and staring at the ceiling, but she saw nothing except stars. She couldn't do more than moan when Jamie slid two fingers against her, slicking herself with the wetness from Deanna's orgasm so she could work her fingers inside Deanna.

At the first press of Jamie's fingers within her, Deanna's limp legs fell back wider, her body opened itself for Jamie.

Though she could still feel the echoes of her last orgasm sparking through her veins, Deanna's hips rose in response to Jamie's questing fingers, urging them deeper. She wanted to feel Jamie everywhere, feel the press of her inside and the warmth of her as she moved over Deanna's body.

Jamie's eyes were dark; her hair was pushed back from her face as she slid her fingers out of Deanna and then in again, twisting until Deanna's fingers scrabbled for purchase against the sheets of her bed.

"Come on, baby," Jamie coaxed, moving her fingers faster until Deanna had to slam her eyes shut. The sensations were too overwhelming for her to do anything but arch up into Jamie, shamelessly begging for more. "I've got you."

Deanna grabbed for Jamie's free hand, and Jamie clenched her fingers tightly around her as she began to fuck Deanna into the mattress. The force of her thrusts let Deanna know that she'd be sore tomorrow, and glad of it. Jamie gave a final twist, her fingers curling over the spot in Deanna that made her vision white out.

When Deanna could think again, she realized Jamie had crawled farther up her body until she straddled Deanna's shoulders. Deanna's lips were just inches from Jamie's clit. Deanna gave a breathless laugh. Her hands slid up Jamie's thighs to bring her closer so that she could bury her face in Jamie, eyes closing as she inhaled the musky scent of her. Jamie was wet, and as Deanna parted her mouth and pressed her lips to the bundle of nerves at the apex of her thighs, Deanna could feel her shudder and her hips rock forward to push herself farther into Deanna's mouth.

Deanna slid her tongue over Jamie's slick skin; her hands moved until she could cup Jamie's ass and feel Jamie push against her in earnest. Jamie took the invitation for what it was. Her movements sped up as she rocked against Deanna's mouth with her hands braced against the back of the couch and sweat beading on her lower back as she fucked Deanna's tongue. Deanna could feel the pressure building between her own legs again, and bucked uselessly against the air, wishing she'd thought to find a pillow or something, anything, to rut against as the fervor of Jamie's movements increased.

Taking her hand from Jamie's ass, Deanna slid it between her own legs, working her fingers desperately against her clit as she sucked Jamie's into her mouth, moaning against her lover when she felt herself come.

The vibration of Deanna's moan against her tipped Jamie over the edge. With a sharp cry she ground herself against Deanna's face, momentarily stealing Deanna's breath. The feeling of Jamie riding her orgasm pressed against Deanna's mouth, with her nose buried in Jamie's curls, had Deanna working her fingers again so that as Jamie came down, easing back so that Deanna could suck in a lungful of air, Deanna was shaking with another orgasm.

Jamie laughed weakly and rolled off of Deanna to fall to the bed beside her. She was sheened with sweat, and as she curled around Deanna, Deanna made a halfhearted attempt to push her away. "Too hot for cuddling," she protested. Her chest was still heaving as she tried to get her breathing under control.

"Never too hot for cuddling," Jamie disagreed, burying her face in Deanna's shoulder and nuzzling closer to her neck. Deanna gave her a halfhearted shove, but didn't have the energy to do more; her skin still thrummed with the afterglow.

"Lesbian bed death, my ass," she muttered drowsily.

"What?"

"Never mind." Deanna gave Jamie's arm, which was slung across her stomach, an absent pat. "Will we need a U-Haul to get my stuff upstairs, do you think?"

"A U-Haul?" Jamie sounded even more confused now, and if Deanna had more energy left she would have laughed.

"Nothing, it's… bad joke."

"I thought that was my domain from now on," Jamie pouted, though Deanna could feel her lips quirk into a grin against the side of her neck.

"We can share," Deanna offered, her tongue thick in her mouth as exhaustion hit. "I want to share a lot of things with you."

"Good." Jamie snuggled closer, lifting the blanket to pull it over them. There was a soft thump, and the bed shuddered, the springs complaining. Deanna didn't have to open her eyes to know that Arthur had joined them, and that he'd be looking guilty about it.

"You're going to spoil him."

"It's sharing, not spoiling." Jamie planted a kiss on Deanna's shoulder. "Plus, you'll have to get used to the idea of puppies in the bed."

"Huh?" Deanna couldn't quite connect the dots there.

"Werewolf." Jamie shrugged, laughter warm in her voice. "You'll get to be a den mother for real."

"Oh, for the love of—" Deanna summoned the rest of her energy and rolled over, trapping Jamie in a kiss that melted into a slow glide of lips and tongue. "You're really not as funny as you think you are."

"But you love me." Jamie smirked.

"Yes." Deanna smiled. "I do."

THE END.

Acknowledgments |

THANK YOU, ELIZABETH, FOR LISTENING to all of my ideas and, more importantly, telling me if they were crap. You were right; this one was pretty good. Thank you, Jonathan, for your unwavering belief in me. Thank you, Leita, Trever, Katelyn and Lowell, for being a community of writers and friends that I'm proud to be a part of. Thank you, Anthony, for giving and asking only for truth. Thank you, Kathryn, who's promised to keep me humble but never stops being excited with me. Thank you to my family, who always encouraged my love of reading and gamely accepted the consequences.

Thank you, Annie, for wanting the best for these characters. Thank you, Candy, for the guiding hand. Thank you, Choi, for making this feel real. Thank you, Lex—I didn't get to know you, but your dream made mine a reality. Thank you, Nicki and Zoe, for your hard work. Thank you, Monika, for the breathtaking cover art.

And thank you fandom. Your love of stories made this possible.

PS: To my fellow Canadians, I apologize for the American spelling. I hope it didn't colour your perception of the book too much.

About the
Author |

MICHELLE OSGOOD WRITES QUEER, FEMINIST romance from her tiny apartment in Vancouver, BC. She loves stories in all mediums, especially those created by Shonda Rhimes, and dreams of one day owning a wine cellar to rival Olivia Pope's. She is active in Vancouver's poly and LGBTQ communities, never turns down a debate about pop culture, and is trying to learn how to cook. *Huntsmen* (2017) and *Moon Illusion* (2018) are the second and third installments of her Better to Kiss You With series.

🌐 interludepress.com
🐦 @InterludePress
📘 interludepress
🛒 store.interludepress.com

interlude press
also by Michelle Osgood...

Huntsmen
The Better to Kiss You With, Book 2

Months after saving Jamie and Deanna from crywolf, Kiara and her brother Cole have moved into the city. While clubbing one night, Kiara is stunned to see her ex, Taryn, onstage. But before she can react, Jamie notices a distinctive tattoo in the crowd: an axe rumored to be the mark of the Huntsmen, a group of werewolf-tracking humans. The girls need to leave immediately—and since Taryn is also a werewolf, they need to take her with them.

The Huntsmen are more than a myth, and they're scouring the city for lone wolves just like Taryn. Until the General North American Assembly of Werewolves lends a plan of action, Kiara's small pack is on lockdown in a friend's apartment, where she and Taryn must face the differences that drove them apart. Furthermore, the longer the group waits, the more it seems the Huntsmen haven't been acting entirely on their own.

ISBN (print) 978-1-945053-19-1 | (eBook) 978-1-945053-33-7

Moon Illusion
The Better to Kiss You With, Book 3

Nathan Roberts was just your average polyamorous librarian living in Vancouver until his best friend Deanna started dating a werewolf. While hosting the small pack in his apartment while they hid from the underground network, the Huntsmen, Nathan gave in to his attraction for Cole, the pack leader's brother. Now, the two are navigating a serious relationship.

When his neighbor is murdered, Nathan is convinced the death is linked to the supernatural, but Cole and their friends deny any paranormal connection. This leads to a fracture of trust between Nathan and Cole, and Cole's pack is left to deal with an unknown killer on the loose. As Nathan pursues answers on his own, he must come to terms with the truth and his feelings for Cole.

ISBN (print) 978-1-945053-56-6 | (eBook) 978-1-945053-57-3